BRAD STEIGER'S OWN STORY

"As some of my readers may know, I grew up in a home in which we had continual paranormal manifestations, ranging from knockings, rappings, the sound of measured footsteps, and occasional materializations.

Among my earliest childhood memories are the man and the woman who would walk into my bedroom at night and stand at my bedside, looking down at me. The man wore a black suit and seemed of rather stern demeanor. The woman wore an old-fashioned dress with a lace collar. Assessing their appearance from photographs I saw much later in an old family album, I have decided that the couple was most likely my great-grandparents, who had lived in the farmhouse long before my birth . . .

These comments are intended to assure you that moving into a house with an unseen resident held no particular terror for me personally; yet, when I moved into a haunted farmhouse with my family, the subsequent occurrences did prove to be quite unsettling . . ."

Berkley Books by Brad Steiger

THE STAR PEOPLE SERIES

THE STAR PEOPLE (with Francie Steiger)
REVELATION: THE DIVINE FIRE
GODS OF AQUARIUS

LIFE WITHOUT PAIN (with Komar)
WORLDS BEFORE OUR OWN
THE UFO ABDUCTORS
MONSTERS AMONG US
GHOSTS AMONG US

Most Berkley Books are available at special quantity discounts for bulk purchases for sales promotions, premiums, fund raising, or educational use. Special books or book excerpts can also be created to fit specific needs.

For details, write or telephone Special Markets, The Berkley Publishing Group, 200 Madison Avenue, New York, New York 10016; (212) 951-8800.

GHOSTS AMONG US

BRAD STEIGER

B
BERKLEY BOOKS, NEW YORK

GHOSTS AMONG US

A Berkley Book / published by arrangement with
the author

PRINTING HISTORY
Berkley edition / May 1990

All rights reserved.
Copyright © 1990 by Brad Steiger.
This book may not be reproduced in whole or in part,
by mimeograph or any other means, without permission.
For information address: The Berkley Publishing Group,
200 Madison Avenue, New York, New York 10016.

ISBN: 0-425-12096-1

A BERKLEY BOOK ®™ 757,375
Berkley Books are published by The Berkley Publishing Group,
200 Madison Avenue, New York, New York 10016.
The name "BERKLEY" and the "B" logo
are trademarks belonging to Berkley Publishing Corporation.

PRINTED IN THE UNITED STATES OF AMERICA

10 9 8 7 6 5 4 3 2 1

Contents

1	Home Is Where the Haunt Is	1
2	Noisy House Busters	33
3	Haunted People	49
4	Entities That Seek to Possess and Destroy	58
5	Phantoms of Fields, Forests, and Shores	72
6	The Eternal Battles of Ghost Armies	85
7	Haunting Styles of the Rich and Famous	98
8	Ghosts on College Campuses	113
9	Chicago—America's Most Haunted City	124
10	Haunted Ground	139
11	Ethereal Advisers and Ghostly Guides	155
Epilogue:	The Enigma of the Ghosts Among Us	179

GHOSTS AMONG US

·1·

Home Is Where the Haunt Is

A Giant, Invisible Rat on a Rampage

On the eve of All Saints' Day in 1972, my associate Glenn McWane, my mediumistic friend Deon Frey, and I answered a call for help from a farm family who had been suffering from ghostly phenomena.

The family in this case consisted of a man and a woman in their mid-twenties and two preschool-age children. In prior interviews and in discussions conducted that evening (before and after a séance held in their kitchen), it would appear that both man and wife had certain mediumistic abilities; both had certain frustrated desires that might have drawn a low-level, external intelligence to them.

Quite early into the séance, after Deon described the entity that both husband and wife had observed on a number of occasions, a combination scratching-gnawing sound began underneath the wooden kitchen table. The sounds grew louder until they reached a volume best described as the vigorous clawing of a two-hundred-pound rat.

As the force of the scratching grew heavier, the tabletop vibrated vigorously. It felt as if something were rubbing itself against my legs, but all five pairs of hands were visible on the tabletop.

The young couple gave no evidence of fear. They had already expressed their confidence in our ability to handle anything that might materialize. Afterward Glenn, Deon, and I confessed that for a time none of us were too certain about what we were up against, but each of us knew better than to feed the thing any high-charged fear.

Our gigantic, "invisible rat" darted out from beneath the table and banged into a cupboard filled with dishes. Although nothing was broken, it sounded as if the thing had smashed every bit of dinnerware the couple possessed.

After a noisy bit of panting, dish rattling, and a few more vigorous scratches, the thing's energy appeared to be severely lessened. It was almost as if, by a joint effort of our wills, that somehow we had been able to reach the entity's cutoff switch. A few more spasmodic scratchings and it was gone and at last report never again has returned.

In this instance both Deon and I had the impression that we were not dealing with a product of human intelligence—nor of anything that had ever been human. The term *nature spirit* came at once to my mind, and Deon tentatively agreed.

I do not know if either of us really knows what we mean by a nature spirit, but perhaps there are pockets of energy or natural forces that can take on vestiges of low-level intelligence. Perhaps for centuries an awareness of such things has impressed upon those who lived close to the land that there are "sacred" areas that must not be violated. These pockets of intelligent energy may be directed and semi-controlled by human intelligence; or, vice versa, that nature spirits direct and semi-control human intelligence.

It's possible that the entity we confronted on Halloween

night, 1972, felt a proprietary interest in that farm. The farmhouse may have been constructed in the very nexus of what to the AmerIndians of the area had long been a "sacred medicine" area. While the ghost may have not intended to harm the young family, consistently it had been scaring the hell out of them.

A Terrible Basement in Nebraska

I first heart of the terrible basement in Lincoln, Nebraska, from a reporter on the *Lincoln Journal and Star*. The image of a bearded man with long, unkempt hair was often seen coming through a wall in the Richard household. What appeared to be blood would ooze from the walls and pour from the faucets near the washing machine.

The man was thought to be the spirit form of the angry husband, who had murdered his wife and her lover with a shotgun and knife in a darkened back room of the basement. The manifestation of blood was the silent commemoration of the violent deed.

When I arrived on the scene with the well-known Chicago medium Irene Hughes, the family had refused to use their basement any longer. The haunting had the mother, and especially the teenaged daughter, on the edge of hysteria.

As the medium, members of the family, and I stood in that eerie back room, Glenn McWane and the reporter observed a strange phenomenon. The door kept trying to close on us.

"See there?" Glenn pointed out. "From the angle at which the door is set, it should naturally swing open. The floor slants a bit, and it would be an uphill fight against gravity for the door to close by itself." But the door had been swinging closed. On two occasions, as the journalist was trying to take a picture of us in the back room, the door had swung nearly shut and had ruined his shot.

Another time Glenn had wedged his toe under the door to hold it open, and it had nearly bent at the top because of the pressure exerted against it.

"All right," I said after Irene had finished receiving impressions from the room. "Shut the darned door if that's what it wants so badly."

Glenn swung the door to close it but found that he had to lift it up to effect a tight fit. "Now the thing should be happy," he said, grinning. "It's closed good and tight."

After Irene Hughes pacified the family about the evil effects of the basement, we walked upstairs to the daughter's room.

"Do you often feel that someone is peeking in that window at you?" she asked Melody.

"All the time!" The teenager shuddered in instant agreement. "It's such an icy feeling!"

Irene moved to a dresser. "There's a strange, almost electrical vibration here," she said.

"We've felt it in the same spot," Mrs. Richard, our frightened hostess, confirmed. "Several friends have felt the same thing there."

"It feels like something moving underneath me," Irene said.

"We've felt it for six years now," Mrs. Richard said.

Just then we were all startled by a loud pounding sound from the basement. It sounded as though a door had been slammed open and that something very heavy and very angry was coming up the stairs with a *Bam! Bam! Bam!*

"It's right under me!" Irene shouted. "It's like somebody

pushing up and banging on the floor. Did everyone feel it and hear it?"

We would've had to have lost feeling below our knees and gone deaf not to have felt and heard the powerful series of knocks.

Glenn and the reporter were already on their way down to the basement. I knew where they were heading, and I walked back to the top of the stairs and shouted down at them: "Well?"

Glenn called up that the door to the back room—the scene of the grisly deaths—was wide open. It appeared that we could not "tame" the presence in the room that easily, since it refused to be locked in by a puny door.

When the two men rejoined us, the journalist said that he had felt a "force" push past him just seconds before the pounding had begun on the floor. Others, who had been standing in a line along the basement stairway said that they, too, had felt "something" rush by them.

The Ugly Man in the Mirror

Irene told us that she was "getting" another image of the spirit in the basement.

Melody spoke up, a tremor slightly warping her voice. "I saw the guy standing behind me when I was combing my hair. He was so ugly that I just smashed the mirror."

Irene continued with her impressions, telling us that the spirit was that of a tall man who was not as ugly as he was unkempt.

Mrs. Richard reentered the conversation by saying they had often seen the man's shadow. "That shadow was the first thing we ever saw in this house that was out of the ordinary. We saw a man's shadow, his outline, in this doorway."

Melody said that seeing the shadow had been a terrible experience. "Every time we see it, I know it's that big, ugly man trying to get us, trying to pull us into the grave with him!" she cried.

The medium walked to a smaller room near the front door and told us she felt a "fast heartbeat" there. "This was the room in which the man was murdered."

The Spirit Kept Returning "Home"

Mrs. Richard reported that they had seen a moving light on some evenings in the room. "We have never been able to explain the light as being caused by any kind of reflection or any light source that we can identify," she said. "It moves across the room from the picture on the wall, to the window, to that light fixture over there."

Irene informed us that this had once been the victim's bedroom, which Mrs. Richard confirmed.

"I feel that his spirit considers this house his home, and that is why he keeps returning here," Irene said. "That is why you have seen his image coming out of the wall. The shadow in the doorway is his image, as if he were coming home from work. And the blood pouring from the faucets is a reminder of the terrible way in which he was murdered. But please understand, this spirit means no one any harm."

After Irene offered a prayer and a meditation for the restless entity's peace, we left the house and entered a garage in the Richards' backyard. It was here, according to most reports, that the maddened husband had put a violent end to his wife with a shotgun blast. The journalist clarified that the body had been dragged to the room in the basement, after the murder. It was a separate crime that had resulted in the stabbing of a man in the same back room where the mangled wife had been deposited by her husband. Irene offered another prayer for all troubled entities that may have been drawn to the scene of this terrible death.

The Richard house, in my opinion, was a kind of "psychic supermarket," an extraordinarily wide range of phenomena coexisting within its walls. There was the strange door that would not stay either open or closed; the ghost of the unkempt man that had appeared in the back room of the basement and in the girl's bedroom; the "blood" that had flowed from the faucet in the basement; and the thumping, thudding "force" that had jarred all of us in the girl's bedroom.

Irene Hughes left the Richard family with instructions as to how they might employ psychic self-defense against any unwanted visitors. She also gave the mother and the daughter private consultations, designed to fortify them against the fear and hysteria that had begun to warp their perspective toward life in the old house.

Although the Richard house basically was haunted, there were certainly strong elements of psychokinetic poltergeist activity. The disturbed teenager, so often an essential ingredient in poltergeist manifestations, was present, but then so were the possibilities of virulent memory patterns having been impressed upon the environment by two murders. The mother and her daughter felt a definite interaction with at least two spirit entities, and Irene seemed to sense and describe them exactly as the women had seen them.

A Haunted Apartment in Wisconsin

Mr. and Mrs. Dennis Smith moved into their apartment in June and found the place perfectly to their liking. Then, in early fall, while his wife was in the hospital having their first child, Dennis had an eerie feeling that someone was standing next to him as he lay dozing on the living-room couch.

He opened his eyes and caught a glimpse of what appeared to be a humanlike shape. When he sat up, it disappeared immediately.

Discounting it as some trick of the eye, Dennis thought no more about the strange illusion.

A Mysterious Form

The next night, just as he was falling asleep in bed, the mysterious form returned. Even though it once again disappeared within brief seconds after its materialization, Dennis was becoming a bit uneasy.

His wife returned from the hospital, and life continued as before for a week or so. Then one night, as he was sitting in a living-room chair, Dennis felt something "burn" him on the right leg.

Neither of the Smiths could offer any explanation for the sensation, but Dennis and his wife agreed that they could sense a "presence"—someone or something in their apartment.

They went to bed early, about nine P.M. and that was when the horror began.

The Powerful Hands of an Unseen Attacker

"I was in bed no longer than ten or fifteen minutes when I felt hands around my throat," Dennis said later.

The powerful hands cut off his breathing, and Dennis grappled desperately with his unseen attacker. With a strength born of panic, he at last managed to tear the hands from his throat.

When he turned on the light, he found the room empty, except for his wife and baby. According to the testimony of the Smiths, there were finger marks on Dennis's neck.

The young couple was seized by terror, and they decided to leave the apartment at once and spend the night in a relative's home.

However, at around eleven-thirty P.M., the Smiths discovered that they had left their apartment in such a hurry that they did not have an adequate supply of clothing for their baby. Summoning their courage, they returned to their home.

A Foglike Shape

Dennis Smith later told Richard Wesnick of the Racine *Journal-Times* that he had seen a "foglike shape" move across the doorway in their bedroom. Dennis described the ghostly fog as resembling something similar to a large ball. His wife described it as "tall, almost humanlike."

Smith called the police department and related his account to a friend on the force, Sylvester Harris. On the next evening Harris accompanied Smith back to the haunted apartment. The two men agreed that Smith would sit alone inside, while Harris stood watch outside.

Then, according to the account in the *Journal-Times*, Smith was seated on a chair next to the television set when he glanced into the bedroom on his left and again saw the form. He jumped up and ran out the front door as Harris ran inside. But there was nothing there. The bedroom was empty and there was no other exit except into the room where the policeman stood.

The Smiths decided that although they didn't really

"believe" in ghosts, they might as well be on the safe side and move. Mrs. Smith testified that she had actually felt something touch her on two different occasions, and the couple had often experienced the uncomfortable sensation that an invisible someone was standing behind them.

Reporter Wesnick talked to Mrs. Veronica Geret, a former resident of the building who had lived there for eleven years, four of which had been spent in the Smith apartment. Mrs. Geret said that she had never experienced anything out of the ordinary, but she commented on the fact that the Smith apartment had been subject to a high turnover of tenants in past years. "They never stay more than a few weeks or months," she told the journalist.

Mrs. Geret said that two young girls had rented the apartment before the Smiths moved in, and they had lived there only about two weeks when they moved out, leaving many of their belongings behind. Mrs. Geret would not say, though, that she believed their brief stay had been due to any haunting or psychic phenomena.

Dennis Smith was not interested in theorizing about what may or may not have been haunting the apartment, and he will always have the memory of those finger marks on his throat.

A Visit From Beyond in Australia

Anita Stapleton, one of my readers from Australia, provided me with the following account, which served to convince her that there exists within us something that survives death. What is more, the inquisitive Ms. Stapleton was able to search out proof of the earthly identity of the

GHOSTS AMONG US

ghost that appeared to her. Following, in her own words, is her very convincing story.

"Is life after death only a matter of religious belief? Is it just wishful thinking? Comfort for the bereaved? Or has it ever been proved?

"These questions pass, at one time or another, through the minds of most people. There have been many stories about visions and apparitions, verbal and written messages from 'beyond.' Are they genuine, or were they caused by imagination, hallucination, self-hypnosis, mental telepathy, or any other form of brainpower?

"As a person with an inquisitive mind, I have reflected upon these questions many times, until one day I received an answer most unexpectedly.

"The day had been a normal one for me in my home in Labrador, Queensland, Australia. I had gone about my daily chores, watched television in the evening, and finally went to bed, while my husband was still watching the late movie on TV.

"The bedroom was not dark, because the bright light of a full moon fell through the window. I had just laid down, ready to go to sleep, when I suddenly noticed that I was not on my own. Right in front of the wardrobe, and looking directly at me—*Good God, what was this?*—was a middle-aged man, dressed like a Catholic priest.

"I rubbed my eyes and pinched my arms to make sure I was fully awake. Yes, I most certainly was. Was I having hallucinations?"

A Ghostly Priest

"The priest was still standing there, looking at me. He was rather a frail man with hollow cheeks. His face showed traces of a hard life and illness. If he had any hair at all, it was covered by his hat.

"He looked so real, not like a ghost. I was not a bit scared, because he radiated vibrations of utter peace and tranquillity. There was nothing to be afraid of.

"I decided to talk to him, keeping my voice as low as possible.

"'Hello, Father,' I said. 'God bless you.'

"'And God bless you, my child,' came the priest's prompt reply. He was well-spoken, his voice soft. His English accent was not hard to distinguish.

"After giving me a few personal messages and stressing the point that there *is* survival after death, he told me who he was. He was Frederick William Faber, and he had lived in England from 1814 to 1863.

"When I remarked that at the time of his passing he was only forty-nine years old, he confirmed this and added that he had died of a kidney disease. After quietly talking about religious matters for a few more minutes, he bade me farewell and disappeared.

"My mind was boggled. As late as it was, it was impossible to think of sleep. I wrote down my unearthly visitor's name and other details. Then I told my husband what had happened.

"Naturally, his first reaction was disbelief and the assertion that I had been asleep and dreaming. Of course, I knew I had been fully awake.

"The whole thing, however, seemed so incredible that doubts came into my mind. The name Faber seemed a bit unusual for an Englishman. Being German, I know quite a few Germans by that name. I recalled a girl, Hildegard Faber, who had gone to school with me. Was this some trickery by my subconscious mind?

"The incident troubled me for days. How could I ever find out the truth?"

In Search of Father Faber

"Then my husband reminded me of Somerset House in London, where a record of every person born and deceased in Britain is kept. However, he did not know how far back these records went. Father Faber, if indeed he had existed, had been dead for over one hundred years.

"Should I write to Somerset House? I hesitated. I did not want to make a fool of myself in case the whole thing was just a hallucination.

"A few days later, however, I took the plunge and wrote to Somerset House, requesting a search. I was sent a form to fill in, giving details of the required person, and was asked to included a small search fee. This I did immediately.

"Now I waited for a reply from Somerset House. This suspense-drama would soon reach its climax. Either I would be told: 'Sorry, there is no record of this person' or . . . I did not dare finish this sentence.

"Two weeks later an airmail letter from London arrived. The sender was Somerset House.

"My hands were shaky. I trembled like a leaf. I was barely able to open the letter. Then I almost fainted.

"The letter contained a certified copy of a death certificate. It stated that Fredrick Will Faber's death had occurred on September 26, 1863 and that he had been forty-nine at the time of his death and had been a doctor of divinity, in Brompton, County of Middlesex. The cause of death was stated as kidney disease. In other words, the official document in my hands confirmed what the apparition had told me.

"If this is not a genuine case of a visit from beyond the grave, what is it? An authority like Somerset House would not send a fictitious document halfway around the world to back up someone's fantasy or hallucination. To the best of my knowledge Father Faber had not been a well-known personality, so books would not have been written about him which I might have read and forgotten about. Nobody alive today is old enough to remember him.

"While it is true that I have been in England, I did not visit any cemeteries there, which rules out the possibility that I may have seen his name on a tombstone. I am absolutely positive that I had never before heard of Father Faber.

"As much as I rack my brain, I cannot find a logical explanation, but I now know for sure that there is life after death. To me it has been proved beyond the shadow of a doubt."

A Haunted Iowa Farmhouse

As some of my readers may know, I grew up in a home in which we had continual paranormal manifestations, ranging from knockings, rappings, the sound of measured footsteps, and occasional materializations.

Among my earliest childhood memories are the man and the woman who would walk into my bedroom at night and stand at my bedside, looking down at me. The man wore a black suit and seemed of rather stern demeanor. The woman wore an old-fashioned dress with a lace collar. Assessing their appearance from photographs I saw much later in an old family album, I have decided that the couple was most likely my great-grandparents, who had lived in the farmhouse long before my birth.

Dimension of spirit had always been very much a part of my mother's life, and she permitted my sister and me to perceive the eerie manifestations as evidence that from time to time a greater reality can impinge upon our more limited physical reality.

These comments are intended to assure you that moving into a house with an unseen resident held no particular terror for me personally; yet, when I moved into a haunted farmhouse with my family, the subsequent occurrences did prove to be quite unsettling.

On the outside, the farmhouse was magnificent. It was a solid two-story dwelling with an inviting front porch and sat atop a grassy hill. It was flanked by majestic pines and backed by a dwindling number of oak and walnut trees, which soon surrendered to a cornfield. At the foot of the hill was a picturesque creek with a small but sturdy bridge. Across the lane from the barn was a cabin said to be one of the very oldest pioneer homes in the county. The sturdy Iowa farmhouse seemed an ideal home in which our family might attempt an experiment in country living.

Inside, however, it seemed another matter entirely. I first entered the home with my friend Komar, who is very psychically sensitive. "Someone died here," he stated bluntly as soon as we crossed the threshold into the dining room.

The woman whose home we were in the process of purchasing appeared startled by my friend's immediate announcement. When Komar quickly added, "A man died in the room across from the kitchen," she became visibly upset.

Within a few days we had the whole story. Her father, who she called Papa, had in his day been a well-respected church and community leader. His "day" had been in the 1920s and 1930s, and he had steadily grown more reclusive and more strongly opposed to modern technology. Papa's distrust of modern times extended to storm windows, electric lights, and running water. Life with Papa had been a rugged existence.

He had yielded to electric lights sometime in the 1940s, and he loved to sit in his room and listen to the radio—one of his few concessions to the contemporary world around him. He had not permitted running water in his house during his lifetime, and the plumbing we now saw had been only recently installed. There still was no drinking water in the home, however, and if we did not wish to carry buckets from the spring near the barn, we would have to dig a well.

A Haunted House of My Own

My objections to the farmhouse were outvoted, and we were soon moving to the country to inhabit Papa's monument to the "good old days." I strongly felt a presence in the house, and I was concerned about the children, since the presence I detected did not seem to be a hospitable one.

Shortly before we were to move in, a cousin of the vacating family approached me with an amused smile. "Well, Brad, you should really be happy now. What more could a writer of all those spooky books want than a haunted house of his own?"

When I pressed him for details, he only shrugged. "The old man was a stubborn Norwegian when he was alive, and I guess he's just as stubborn now that he's passed on. You should have some interesting evenings ahead of you."

I evaluated the situation, and we had a problem. If we truly were dealing with the earthbound spirit essence of a man who had been a pious church leader and a fervent opponent of progress, just how would he take to a family moving into his home that was headed by a psychical investigator with four lively kids who would immediately begin playing stereos and television sets? And how would the impressionable psyches of the kids, aged eight to sixteen, respond if the spirit became antagonized?

I was the first to undergo an initiation at the hands of an invisible welcoming committee.

I was alone in the house on a Sunday morning having some tea and toast while I read the newspaper. My wife, Marilyn [who died in 1982], had gone to the village to open the small retail store she managed. One moment things were as idyllic as they could be; the next, my tranquillity was shattered by a violent explosion that seemed to come from the basement.

Spectral Explosions

Fearing that the oil-burning furnace had somehow exploded, I opened the basement door, expecting the worst. I could hear what seemed to be the walls of stone and brick caving in on the washer, the dryer, and the other appliances. I expected to be met by billowing clouds of thick black smoke.

But the instant I stepped onto the basement landing, all sounds of disturbance ceased. The furnace was undamaged. The walls stood firm and solid. There was no smoke or fire.

Before I could puzzle the enigma through, I was startled by the sound of yet another explosion coming from somewhere upstairs. I had a terrible image of the old brick chimney collapsing, and then I was pounding my way up the stairs.

The attic was as serene as the basement had been. I shook

my head in confusion as I studied the sturdy beams and the excellent workmanship that held the roof and the brick chimney firmly erect and braced. The house had been built by master carpenters and bricklayers. It could probably withstand a tornado, I thought to myself as I attempted to understand what was happening around me.

A massive eruption sounded from the basement again, creating the visual image of several hand grenades being triggered in rapid succession. I slammed the attic door behind me, fearing the awesome damage that surely must have occurred.

But before I could run back down the stairs to inspect the extent of the destruction, I heard what sounded like someone tap-dancing behind the door to my son Steven's room. I knew that Steven did not tap-dance and that I was home alone.

Then I thought of Reb, our beagle. I laughed out loud in relief. The sound of "tap dancing" had to be the clicking of the dog's paws on the wooden floor. But why wasn't Reb barking to be released? He was never shy about expressing his wishes, frustration, or irritation.

I hesitated with my hand on the doorknob. I felt an even greater hesitation when I heard Reb barking *outside*. The dog was out back, by the kitchen door. I was so engrossed in the mystery of the strange disturbances that I had forgotten I had let him out. It was cold that morning, and Reb was barking to come into the warm house.

Who—*what*—was still merrily dancing behind the door to Steven's room?

I shamed myself for permitting fear to make me lose control of my hand. I twisted the knob and pushed open the door.

The room was empty. And the dancing stopped as

GHOSTS AMONG US

suddenly as the explosions had when I had swung aside the basement and attic doors.

I suddenly felt as though I were being scrutinized by a dozen or more pairs of eyes.

Another detonation roared up at me from the basement.

A Silly Game With Unseen Pranksters

I sensed a game plan behind all of this. I was now supposed to dash down the stairs in puzzled panic, desperately seeking the cause of the violent "explosion." I could almost hear the giggles of unseen pranksters.

I resolved not to play the silly game anymore. I walked purposefully back to the kitchen table, where I had left my tea, toast, and Sunday newspaper.

Then it sounded as if the attic roof were being torn from its anchoring beams. The basement walls shuddered and collapsed in what seemed to be another explosion.

During my career as a psychical researcher I had become well versed in the games that certain entities like to play with people. I decided to do my best to ignore the phenomena.

The tap dancing was nearer now. It was coming from the music room, the room that the previous owners had kept locked and unused—Papa's room. I had placed the piano, television, and stereo in the room and had repainted the walls and the ceiling. I had blessed the room and announced that it would henceforth be a place of love and laughter.

I was determined not to glance up from my newspaper, even if Papa, a headless horseman, or a snarling troll came walking out of the music room. I was not going to play the game.

Within about twenty minutes the disturbances had stopped. I was relieved that I had guessed the secret. It appeared that the invisible pranksters did not enjoy playing tricks on someone who remained indifferent to such a grand repertoire of mischief.

Since I did not wish to alarm the rest of the family and was totally immersed in working on a new book at my office in the village, I did not mention the incident to anyone.

The Tricksters Strike Again

About three nights later, when I was working late at my office, I received an urgent telephone call from my older son, Bryan. The panic in the sixteen-year-old's voice told me that I must drive out to the farmhouse at once.

When I arrived, I found Bryan barricaded in his room, together with Reb and a .12-gauge shotgun. After I had calmed the boy I learned that Bryan, too, had fallen victim to the tricksters.

Bryan had been alone at home watching television in the music room. He heard what he assumed was the sound of other family members returning home. He listened to the familiar noises of an automobile approaching, car doors slamming, voices and laughter, and the stomping of feet on the front porch.

Then he was surprised to hear loud knocking at the front door. Everyone in the family had their own keys, so why would anyone knock? And why would they be pounding at the front door when they usually entered through the back door, in the kitchen.

Bryan begrudgingly stirred himself from his television program and went to admit whoever was on the front porch. He was astonished to find it empty.

Just as he was about to step outside in an attempt to solve the mystery, he heard knocking at the back door. Uttering a sigh of frustration, Bryan slammed the front door and began

GHOSTS AMONG US

to head for the kitchen. He had taken no more than a few steps when the knocks were once again at the front door.

By now Bryan knew that someone was playing a joke on him. He turned on the yard light so that he could identify the jokesters' automobile. He gasped when he saw that his car was the only one there.

Fists were now thudding on both doors, and Reb was going crazy, growling and baring his teeth.

Bryan next became aware of an eerie babble of voices and short bursts of laughter. Someone very large was definitely leaning against the kitchen door, attempting to force it open.

That was when he called me. A few seconds of hearing my son's strained, frightened voice and the angry snarls of the dog in the background convinced me that something was very wrong.

"Dad," Bryan told me, "Reb and I are in my room. Someone is coming up the stairs. I can hear him move up one step at a time!"

An intuitive flash informed me what was occurring. The invisible pranksters were playing games again.

"Bry, your fear is feeding it," I advised my son. "It has already tried the game with me. Try to stay calm. Put on some music. Distract your mind. I'm on my way home right now!"

It had snowed earlier that day, and I prayed for no ice and no highway patrolman. I was fortunate in both respects and managed to shave four minutes from the normal twelve-minute drive to the farmhouse.

The doors were locked from the inside, and Bryan was still barricaded in his room with Reb. I offered silent thanks that the boy hadn't blown any holes in himself or the walls with the shotgun.

I showed Bryan that there were no footprints in the

freshly fallen snow. There was no evidence of tire tracks in the lane. No human had visited him, I explained, but rather some nonphysical intelligences that would initiate a spooky game with anyone who would play along with them.

How Best to Deal With Ghosts

Early the next evening I gave my children instructions on how best to deal with any ghostly mechanisms of sound or sight that might frighten them.

Basically the strategy was to remain as indifferent and as aloof to the disturbances as possible. In a good-natured way one should indicate that he or she simply does not wish to play such silly games.

Under no circumstances should one become defiant or angry or threatening. The laws of polarity would only force the tricksters into coming back with bigger and spookier tricks in response to the negative energy that had been directed toward them.

Whether we were dealing with poltergeists, restless spirits in limbo, or a repository of unknown energy that somehow mimicked human intelligence, I felt that I had given the kids some advice that was sound.

Bryan had experienced the phenomenon firsthand, so he was now better prepared to confront it should the situation arise. Steven had already intellectualized the occurrences and found them fascinating. My daughter, Kari, who had strong mediumistic abilities, seemed aware of the disturbances but remained strangely aloof from them.

Julie and the Weird Music

It was all a little too awesome for eight-year-old Julie to understand however. Whenever she was left alone in the farmhouse, the entities would gang up on her, and I would return to find her standing at the end of the lane or seeking refuge in a neighbor's home. In each instance she complained of having heard strange voices, laughter, and weird music.

One night, just as I entered my office, I heard the telephone ringing. It was Julie. She had been calling the office ever since I had left home and was in tears. A dramatic manifestation had begun within minutes after I had left her at the kitchen table, eating cookies and drinking milk.

This time it had begun with laughter from the music room. There was a noisy blur of voices, as if several people were trying to speak at once. Then came some "funny piano music" and the sound of a drum.

Valiantly Julie had tried to practice what I had told her to do: to remain calm, act aloof, and not to play the game with whatever it is that likes to play such spooky tricks on people.

When the rhythmic tapping of the drum suddenly gave way to blaring horns and trumpets, Julie's indifference melted.

I had not been gone for more than two or three minutes, but Julie knew that I was headed for the office. She just let the telephone ring until I answered it.

Not long ago Julie, now twenty-three, and I recalled the incidents that she had experienced in the eerie old farmhouse. Interestingly enough, Julie finally had identified the music she had heard coming from the music room on the several occasions she had been left alone.

"When I was a senior in high school," she said, "some girlfriends and I were just driving around one night, and we had on one of those radio stations that play nostalgic music from the 'good old days.' We were talking about how different some of the music used to be, when suddenly I just about freaked out. It was a good thing that I wasn't driving! It was the same music that I had heard coming from that spooky room, and all those terrible memories came back to me."

Julie had heard Glenn Miller's "In the Mood."

Incredibly it had been music from the 1940s that had so frightened Julie. To this day, whenever she hears Benny Goodman, Duke Ellington, or Glenn Miller, she gets a cold shiver, for it was their old records that she had heard playing from the darkened recesses of the music room.

Although she grew up in a home where we enjoyed eclectic musical taste, I must confirm that the tunes of the 1940s would have been foreign to Julie at that time of her life. The family had classical, folk, motion-picture themes, rock, pop, and Broadway show tunes, but we had no big-band records from the 1940s in our collection.

Now that she was older, I shared with Julie what I knew about the music room. Papa had been a strong-willed man who didn't care much for progress—not even running water in the house. And he never would have approved of his daughter and her husband selling the place. He had died in that room, and they had kept it locked and had never used it again while they lived there, since things just hadn't felt right in there.

Papa might not have cared much for most of the instruments of progress, but he must have accepted radio. And he probably tolerated the music of the 1940s, the years when he would have been having some of the most meaningful experiences of his life.

Or maybe the invisible tricksters just loved to jitterbug.

Ghostly Phenomena in an Old House in Michigan

The following account (circa 1968) was prepared for me by the political writer Russell Kirk, through the suggestion of my friend Steve Yankee. The first-person narrative voice is Kirk's.

"For four generations my family's house on the edge of the village of Mecosta, in the old lumbering country of Michigan, has been disturbed—or embellished—by what commonly are called ghostly phenomena. But as I tell my young wife, Annette, 'The darkness belongs to us.' There seem to be ghosts of the sort that William Butler Yeats evoked to guard an infant son.

"The house, a pleasant, bracketed, foursquare Victorian building, was erected in 1878 by my great-grandfather, Amos Johnson. One of his daughters, Miss Norma Johnson, now eighty-nine, still lives here with us, and never has lived anywhere else. The house was occupied for most of its history by women—my great-grandmother, Estella Johnson, widowed at the turn of the century, and her two spinster daughters, Frances and Norma. (I bought the place from an uncle in 1955.) It was never considerably altered, internally or externally, although I am compelled to make some structural repairs just now.

"In my great-grandmother's time the whole family, and a circle of friends, were Spiritualists and Swedenborgians."

A House of Séances

"Many séances were held in the house—and those influences seem to linger. My great-aunt Norma still tells of table levitation, dim wraiths, and ominous sounds produced at the nocturnal sessions in the front parlor, and things still odder. My great-grandmother apparently was a medium of some power and, on one occasion, was raised up toward the ceiling upon the handsome round table that still sits in that parlor.

"One enthusiast frequently came to the house with a guitar. He could not play his instrument, but sometimes it floated independently in the tall parlor, played by invisible hands. An eminent member of this circle was Woodbridge Ferris, founder of Ferris Institute at Big Rapids, and later United States senator and governor of Michigan. He most earnestly desired to communicate with the dead but never succeeded.

"The grimmest of these séances had to do with a murder in the 1880s. My great-grandfather's uncle, Giles Gilbert, was the lumber baron of these parts, and my great-grandfather and his brothers were employed by him. One of those brothers, sent out on a Saturday to pay off the lumberjacks in the camps, did not return that night and could not be found the next day. On Sunday evening my great-grandfather and some others sat around the table in the parlor in the dark, seeking a sign.

"After some time my great-grandfather, a tall man with a red beard, muttered, 'I see him.' He described a spot in the forest where his brother lay facedown. When the men went to look, his brother's body was found, shot through the head, the payroll money he was carrying gone.

"Perhaps the most curious manifestation in this circle of believers was the writing on the slates. Pairs of wood-framed slates were placed face-to-face during séances, and writing would appear on the inner faces. Today, while cleaning the attic, I came upon these very slates, preserved for eighty years. There are three pairs, and they still bear writing, allegedly that of dead people, members of the family, at a famously successful séance.

"The principal ghostly authors are my other great-grandfather, Isaac Pierce (who went out to California in Gold Rush days), and his mother, Eliza Porter Pierce. For the most part, this handwriting is clear. The messages are brief and are written to assuage grief. The purported authors write of being happy and free from pain. My grandfather, Frank Pierce, then a boy, was told to study diligently. On one slate Isaac Pierce wrote in orange, blue, and yellow—the colors of the carpet that then lay on the parlor floor. Those colors remain bright on the slate today, although the carpet long ago went to its own Limbo.

"Of the members of this Spiritualist circle, one of the more intense was Jerome Wilcox, who lived next door. He swore that if it were in any way possible, after his death he would make himself known to his friends. The night he died, some knocks were heard on the head of a bed in my great-grandfather's house—but nothing conclusive.

"My great-grandmother Johnson, Gah, lived to be about ninety-two, rarely leaving this house. Every night after dinner she would retire to her room to read—and to communicate with her dead friends. (Only when I was grown was I informed of this habit of Gah's.) At her death, thirty years ago, the last of the adult generation of Mecosta seekers who experimented with the occult vanished from our village. But the ghostly phenomena did not totally cease."

Faces at the Window

"My own most dramatic glimpse of something uncanny occurred when I was about nine years old. I had come to Mecosta for the Christmas holidays. At the time my parents and I lived in Plymouth, Michigan. Because the house was crowded, I was put to bed on a sofa in the front parlor, where the séances were once held.

Taking off my glasses, I slid into my improvised bed. I noticed that there were something outside the panes of the large bay window across the room. Two men appeared to be looking in, though there was deep snow outside. One man was tall, with a beard and a tall hat; the other was short and wore a roundish hat.

Thinking that this must be some sort of optical illusion, I put my glasses back on. But the two men still were there. Could this be the branch of some tree near the window? I could have gone up close to the panes or hurried out the door and around the house to see who the men might be, but both these being uncomfortable prospects, I drew my head under the covers and went to sleep.

"The next morning when I went outside, I found no footsteps in the snow, nor any branch near the window. Considerably impressed, I did not mention this apparition to anyone.

"Not until many years later did I learn that my Aunt Fay had had similar experiences when she was a child living in Mecosta. She used to play, she tells me, outside the house, near the parlor's bay windows. As very small children sometimes do, she had two male friends with whom she conversed and who no one else ever saw. Their names were Pati and Dr. Cady. Dr. Cady was tall, with a beard, and wore a tall hat. Pati was short and wore a turban."

Rappings and Tricky Lights

"Over the decades the haunting phenomena have been observed at what we call the Old House. For some years I was the only member of the family who would willingly sleep upstairs. The large bedroom over the front parlor was a particularly uneasy spot. Now and again, inexplicable knockings were heard on the headboard of my great-grandfather's tall Victorian bed, as well as footsteps on the stairs. Ten years ago, as I slept in that bed, I was violently awakened by what seemed to be the rattling of a bunch of keys against the door of the room, but when I leapt out of bed, I found no one. During the past month, my wife, sleeping alone there while I was away on lecture tours, was mightily disturbed one night by eight successive raps on the headboard, all in the space of a few seconds. The raps recurred several times during the night.

"We also have the problem of the electric lights. Electrical wiring was installed upstairs only about thirteen years ago. My great-aunt Frances, now dead, who hated all innovation, strongly objected, in her silent way, to this modernism. She was then on the verge of senility but still strong-willed. For a year after the lighting was installed, from time to time all the lights upstairs would fail—through no cause that an electrician could find. Certainly, in her state of health, my great-aunt Frances could not have scurried into the cellar and fiddled with the fuses and switches. After her death the lights behaved decently again. If ever a house was haunted by a living presence, it was ours—and the presence was our brooding great-aunt Frances.

"One summer two Scottish boys were my guests upstairs. Henry Lorimer was roused in the middle of the night by a feeling of oppression and dread. He saw an old, old woman standing in the middle of the room, but she vanished when he sprang up. I suspect the wraith to have been Frances Johnson, then very near to death but still nominally among the living. According to studies made by the Psychical Research Society, the most frequently encountered apparition is one of a person about to die or who had been dead only a few minutes or hours."

Jerome Wilcox's Passion for Immortality

"I have already mentioned my great-grandparents' neighbor, Jerome Wilcox, a humorous and amiable man who was deeply involved in the occult circle. His pledge to return after death appeared to have gone unfulfilled for a great while. Yet it seems he enjoyed a certain success a generation later.

"By 1937, my mother was one of the few people who remembered Jerome, whom we called uncle. She had told me about Wilcox and his passion for ghostly immortality. The following incident occurred in our house at Plymouth, nearly two hundred miles southeast of Mecosta. Since it happened sometime in 1937, it was somewhat startling to both of us.

"I was reading in the living room of our house. My mother was in the kitchen, and my sister, about eleven years old, was with some very young friends, manipulating a Ouija board on the dining-room table. The board's indicator began to move abruptly, and the girls called out to my mother, 'Margie, what is it spelling?'

"'What are the letters?'" she inquired.

"'J-e-r-o-m-e,'" they spelled out. The little girls did not recognize this as a name. The Ouija board revealed no more.

"In 1964 I was back at my house in Plymouth, getting a large quantity of family papers out of the attic. As I dragged the last chest of papers toward the stairs, I noticed behind me, in the dust of the attic floor, a folded piece of paper. Although many scraps of paper were on the attic floor, on some impulse I went back and picked up this particular one.

"I put it in my pocket and examined it a few hours later. It turned out to be a letter, cleverly folded so as to present eight equal sides, written in a sardonic and amusing fashion, about people at Mecosta around 1890. There was no signature. The next day I asked my Aunt Fay to identify the writer, if possible. She examined the sheet: 'Oh, that's Jerome Wilcox's writing.' Why had this come to my hand after so many years, two hundred miles from Mecosta?

"Later I bought the small house where Jerome Wilcox and his wife had once lived. Since I acquired that property, odd articles that had belonged to Wilcox have inexplicably been turning up; an autograph book, a letter, and the like. I've not yet slept in his little house, though. Can it be that old Jerome finds me the only likely person to whom evidence of ghostly durability might be presented?"

Chance Encounters With Ghosts

"I offer no general theory to account for these phenomena in my own house, except to suggest that strong intellectual and emotional experiences tend to linger. I do not know whether the manifestations at Mecosta will endure beyond the approaching death of my surviving great-aunt, Norma Johnson, the last person who serves as a link with the experiments of the 1880s and 1890s.

"Although the irregular, unpredictable, and fragmentary incidents mentioned above tend to frighten some visitors to our house, and even to disquiet some members of the family, I never have been overly disturbed or even passionately interested in them. If anything is at work, it does not seem harmful, and there is no very clear indication of consciousness in these 'presences.' So far as they communicate anything, it is simple admonition or information, even in the most satisfying séances of the old era.

"At one session, for instance, the ghost of George W. Johnson, a brother of my great-grandfather, apparently made himself known. Uncle George had been killed, or at least had disappeared totally, in the Civil War. When asked how he had died, he replied, by slate writing, 'I was shot, shot, shot.' There is indeed some historical evidence suggesting that he was obliterated in a barrage.

"One afterthought: My assistant, William Odell, is an expert in handwriting analysis. He has examined our family 'spirit slates,' and on the six of them he finds that the writing still remaining is in at least three different hands. This fact seems to diminish the possibility that the visiting medium under whose ministrations the writing appeared was merely a charlatan. Nevertheless, the messages themselves are of no great interest and amount to little more than standard communication from beyond.

"The continuity of family, building, and even furniture in my Mecosta house presumably favors the faint survival of traces of a vanished consciousness. It reminds me of Santayana's theory that emotion may imbed itself in matter, to be detected long after by another consciousness under peculiar conditions of receptivity.

"I have no desire to exorcise. If the ghosts will tolerate me, I will tolerate them."

• 2 •

Noisy House Busters

"There it is again," Eric Moulton said with a groan, indicating the loud scratching noise that had begun in their attic. "The blasted ghost is having his jollies."

Mrs. Moulton winced as what sounded like a heavy trunk was slammed on the floor above her. "I wish he could be a bit quieter, love." She sighed. "But at least he never stays at it too long."

Eighteen-year-old Michael, Moulton's stepson, walked into the living room where his parents sat attempting to watch television above the noise of the thumping, bumping ghost in the attic.

"The bloody thing is at it again, is it?" He shrugged, seating himself before the set. "What's on the telly tonight?"

The Moulton home in Middleton, England, had been plagued by the noisy ghost for several years. The thing always began by scratching around in the attic like some wild beast, then it would slam an occasional door, and sometimes move down into the Moultons' living quarters and shove around a few pieces of furniture. The Moultons had learned to live with their pesky spook, until that night in mid-January when Mr. Moulton put forth a proposition that had recently occurred to him.

"I'm thinking of seeing Father Murphy to find out if he could come and exorcise the bloody thing!" he said.

"What's that?" his wife, Dorothy, asked. She couldn't hear him over the sound of something banging the floor in the attic directly above her. "You want to have Father Murphy for supper?"

"No, I'm thinking of having Father Murphy come to exorcise the bloody spook!"

"You mean, say prayers for its restless soul and send it on its way?" Dorothy wondered.

"That's right," Moulton answered resolutely.

"Whatever you think best, love," she told him, then turned her attention back to the television program.

Moulton may have thought at the time that he had made a wise decision, but to his great regret his determination to exorcise the attic spook turned out to be the worst decision he could have reached.

The Reverend Frank Murphy, of St. Mary's Church in Middleton, came to their home on January 20, 1968, prepared to "lay" the ghost to rest. Father Murphy performed the rites of exorcism and told the Moultons not to worry about their rambunctious spirit any longer.

"Well, my dear," Moulton told his wife that night as they prepared to go to bed, "that should be that. Our playful spook has been sent packing."

"Good Lord!" Dorothy shouted, pointing toward the doorway, "then what is that?"

A misty black form hovered in the doorway of the bedroom, then drifted up toward the attic.

Exorcism Only Made the Ghost Angry

That night, instead of the scratching and tapping, the Moultons were bombarded with great bangings in the walls and what appeared to be the sound of heavy feet stomping throughout their three-bedroom, two-story home.

"Uh-oh, my pet," Moulton said as he lay next to his wife in their double bed, "you don't suppose we've angered the thing by calling in the priest, do you?"

When Dorothy Moulton returned from an errand the next day, she found that all the clothes in her bedroom closet had been pulled out and thrown around the room.

"Can't be the spook," her husband argued. "He's never done anything mean before."

But in the ensuing days the Moultons found their dresser drawers ripped out and their contents strewn all over the floor. Their beds were pulled apart, and it became impossible to keep their clothes in the closets.

"It must be someone playing a mean joke on us," Moulton said, stubbornly defending the ghost. "I mean, the spook has always stayed with scratching and knocking."

"That's true," Michael said, "but that was before you decided to call in the priest to chase the ghost out of the attic!"

"But see here, now," Moulton said, producing several thick rolls of tape from a paper bag. "Today, before we go out, I'm going to tape up every window and door in the house with this. That way, even if the tape doesn't keep the cruel jokesters out of the house, at least we'll be able to prove to ourselves whether or not it is the ghost doing all these nasty things."

The Spook Plays Mean

When the Moultons returned that night, they found several rooms in their house completely upset. Clothing, furniture, and kitchen utensils had been dumped on the floor. Not a single inch of the tape had been disturbed.

Carolyn Fleetham, a twenty-year-old typist who rented a room from the Moultons for a time, remembered seeing an apparition outside the bathroom door.

"It was a white, misty shape," she said, "and it looked like a disconnected head! I was just coming out of the bathroom when I saw it."

"I never believed in ghosts," she added, "but now I'm not so sure." Miss Fleetham's belief did, however, grow to the extent where she moved out of the Moulton home.

Michael nearly left the family nest because of the ghost, but he decided not to desert his mother and stepfather.

"It's getting me down, though," he said at the time. "I've never actually seen the ghost, but the sounds the blasted thing makes are bad enough.

"It's especially bad at night when we're trying to settle down to rest," he emphasized. "I can hear the noise of the thing scratching away, and then there are the footsteps that clomp around all night."

Michael acknowledged that the haunting was not quite so bad on him because he was at work all day.

"But I'm terribly worried over the effect the spook is having on my stepmother, Dorothy," he said. "That thing keeps pounding away all night, and we can't get a decent night's sleep. I'm afraid Dorothy is facing a nervous breakdown over the bloody ghost."

Father Murphy expressed concern that his blessing of the

ghost had had such a negative and violent effect on the paranormal prankster.

"I'm truly sorry that things have become worse for the Moultons," the clergyman was quoted as saying. "But I assure you that it is not normal for such things to happen after a blessing. The Moultons are good, simple folks, and I fully believe all that they have told me about the manifestations in their home."

A "Genuine" Ghost

Another person who researched the phenomena and came away a believer in the manifestations was John Daly of the Psychic Research Society of Manchester. Daly testified that he had spent a night in the Moulton residence, and he said that he, too, had heard the same ghostly noises. Daly quickly qualified his remarks by stating that he had first investigated for any evidence that the Moultons might have been faking the dramatic displays of their ghostly lodger.

"We always check for any possible form of fraud in cases such as these," he said, "but this business at the Moulton home seems to be a genuine ghost. The haunting is really quite extraordinary, and we can find no cause for the happenings."

Extensive research could produce no reason why the Moultons should have been so afflicted by a reckless denizen from another dimension. The house itself had been built in 1955 as a farmhouse. The farmer who had worked the land died in 1963. There is no evidence to support the contention that the spirit of the farmer might be attempting to reclaim his home from the Moultons.

Although the violent eye of the psychic storm in the Moulton house eventually spent its preternatural energy and was reabsorbed into the cosmos, the Moulton family of

Middleton, England, would always be able to tell a convincing tale to even the most skeptical audience that they had indeed had a strange encounter with a ghost.

The Ghost That Traveled Over My Telephone Line

The voice on the telephone was warped by confusion, tension, and fear. The young man, called Jim, could not believe that such nightmarish experiences were actually happening to him.

It all began for Jim and his finacée, Carol, while he was investigating UFO sightings in their home state. On one occasion Carol had accompanied Jim and other researchers. During the course of one evening's mysterious activities, she had somehow entered a trancelike state.

Later, in a strange dream, grotesque entities told Carol that they wanted her. She must leave Jim because he was wrong for her, they said. If she did not join them, they would have Jim killed. The dreams continued, becoming more violent and terrifying as the nights progressed.

Because Jim knew of my experience in dealing with ghosts and other mysterious entities, he made a desperate long-distance telephone call to get my advice on how to free Carol from the apparent spell of the phenomenon.

First of all, I assured Jim that such manifestations never appeared to be physically harmful. Frightening and threatening, indeed—but not actually harmful. Some witnesses had reported suffering black or red eyes after an encounter, but that appeared to be connected with the peculiar electromagnetic aspect of the phenomenon rather than any real physical violence.

The important thing, I told Jim, was not to play the

entities' game, and especially not to cast them in the role of evil. It is this dualistic concept that comes so readily to humankind that sets up the warfare structure with the phenomenon. If you permit hostility, then that is what you will receive.

I told Jim that in my opinion, the phenomenon was neither good nor evil. How the entities conduct themselves depends, in large part, on the human being with whom they interact. Cry out in fear and they'll give you good reason to fear them.

I told him I was convinced that this aspect of the larger phenomenon has been constructed primarily as a teaching mechanism. Anyone who finds himself or herself the victim of negative aspects of the phenomenon must at once begin restructuring reality, *excluding* the entities and breaking their hold on his or her mental construct of what is real.

I sent Jim a letter in which I presented a number of specific guidelines for dissipating the poltergeist activity that had been afflicting Carol.

My spoken and written advice seemed to provide Jim and Carol with the kind of support they needed, and the phenomenon around them appeared to decrease.

An Entity Invades My Office

Satisfied that I had been able to assist Jim and Carol, I thought back to an earlier time when I had endured a number of poltergeisic plundering of my own office.

One night as I sat at my typewriter, I heard heavy footfalls at the top of the stairs. A quick glance told me that no one was there. Then a favorite painting of Edgar Allan Poe fell to the floor, and I became irritated.

Papers began to rustle off to my side. A single sheet became airborne.

I'd had enough. A few nights before, several books had launched themselves from their shelves and piled up in the middle of the floor.

I looked up from my typewriter, rolled my eyes upward in disgust, and shouted, "Just cut it the hell out!"

Everything stopped.

I experienced that peculiar sensation one feels when one walks into a crowded, noisy room and everyone suddenly stops talking. I went back to my writing without further notice of anything but the work at hand.

It would seem that every kind of intelligence—regardless of how high or how low—wishes to be recognized. Nothing deters the activity of any thinking entity faster than ignoring it.

Of course, I hadn't really ignored the invisible prowler. I had commanded the poltergeistlike force. I had refused to go along with its framework of reality, and my own change of attitude—from passive fear to rage—apparently had done the trick. I had served notice that I would no longer play the game.

The cessation of activity in my office had been so abrupt that it was very much like the termination of some kind of lesson, some kind of testing process. Evidently I had passed with satisfactory marks.

Haunting by Long-distance

A few nights after I last heard from Jim I received another panicked call from him. The force had returned. Even now it was thudding the walls of their apartment.

The long-distance line was able to transmit the sounds very clearly. Carol was whimpering in the background.

I kept repeating that they must remain calm. I assured them that they could stand firm against the phenomenon and resist it. I leaned back in my chair and reached for the book I had been reading.

Thud! Thud! The first hammering sounds came from the ceiling. *Thud! Thud!* The next blows vibrated the wall near a bookcase.

The poltergeist's energy had traveled along the telephone line and was now manifesting in *my* office. Somehow the frequency of the disturbances had been transmitted well over a thousand miles.

Several books began to dislodge themselves from their shelves. The powerful thudding sounds seemed to echo from wall to wall.

I must confess that it took every ounce of my mental resolve and emotional reserve to stay in that office during the first few moments of the sudden and unexpected poltergeisic onslaught. My mind boggled at the thought that the chaotic energy had used the telephone system to transport itself from Jim's apartment to my office.

I practiced a bit of yogic breathing to calm myself, then I practiced what I had been preaching to Jim and Carol. I refused to play the game. I asserted my control of the situation and I did not show fear.

When I left my office later that evening, the disturbances had ceased. With a great effort of will I held my psychic ground.

And it appears that the poltergeist energy had spent itself, since I received no more distressful telephone calls from Jim and Carol.

What Is a Poltergeist?

Although the poltergeist, that racketing bundle of projected repression, is usually associated with a youth entering puberty who is trying to define his or her sexual role, such psychokinetic disturbances as the levitation of crockery and furniture and the materialization of voices and forms have been reported among newlyweds during the period of marital adjustment. The late psychoanalyst, Dr. Nandor Fodor, believed that the human body is capable of releasing energy in an unconscious and uncontrolled manner, thereby providing the power for the poltergeist's pranks.

In his book, *Poltergeists*, author Sacheverell Sitwell agreed that the psychic energy for such disturbances usually comes from the psyche of someone undergoing sexual trauma. "The particular direction of this power is always toward the secret or concealed weaknesses of the spirit . . . the obscene or erotic recess of the soul," Sitwell conjectured.

If two young people who are experimenting with the regenerative life force and learning to adjust to each other's sexual desires and needs are truly transmitting all sorts of powerful vibrations, then it might seem within the realm of possibility that certain life-force waves might in some way reactivate old memory patterns that have permeated "haunted" rooms. At the same time these sensual shock waves might stimulate the activity of certain shadowy entities best left undisturbed.

A Haunted Honeymoon

Should the reader be willing to accept the thesis that two young people in the throes of marital adjustment are capable of setting certain paranormal phenomena into psychokinetic motion, then one can imagine the phenomena that might be produced by *three* newlywed couples living under the same roof. Author M. G. Murphy provided the editors of *Fate* magazine with a notarized affidavit certifying the authenticity of the eerie events described by the six participants of such a haunted honeymoon.

The Murphys (author Murphy's parents), the Nelsons, and the Chapmans found themselves with a common problem in February 1917: the scarcity of money. They decided to find a house large enough so that each couple would have their own bedroom, then cut down on expenses by sharing the rent. After a period of house hunting, they found an immense three-story house on the outskirts of Santa Ana, California, which rented for an absurdly small sum.

Mrs. Murphy was an avid student of antiques, and she was overwhelmed by the splendid treasures the house contained. It seemed incredible that one could even consider renting out such a magnificent house complete with such valuable antiques, but the three young couples were not about to argue with Providence.

Sounds of Steps on the Stairs

A few days after they moved in, the three young wives were interrupted while polishing the paneled doors by the sound of someone running up the stairs. They had the full length of the stairway in their sight, yet they could only hear the unmistakable sounds of someone clomping noisily up the stairs. Their report of the incident that night at dinner brought tolerant smiles from their husbands.

Several nights later the household members were jolted out of their sleep by Mrs. Nelson screaming that something was trying to smother her. While her husband sat ashen-faced with fear she wrestled with an invisible assailant, until finally she was thrown to the floor with such force that her ankle twisted beneath her and her head hit the wall.

The doctor who was called to treat Mrs. Nelson's injuries mumbled something about it not being surprising considering the house they were living in and would say no more.

Within the next few days the footsteps continued to sound up and down the stairway. The men heard them, too, and they also heard slamming doors and the splashing of water faucets being turned on.

One night everyone saw the huge sliding doors pushed open by an invisible hand, and they all felt a cold breeze blow past them. When they locked the doors that night, one of the men observed that they were really locking up to protect the outside world from what they had on the inside. He was rewarded for his flippant observation by an incredibly foul, nauseating odor that hung around the stairway for days.

The three couples held a council to decide whether or not they should move. Although the disturbances were somewhat annoying, they reasoned, the rent simply could not be beat. They would bear the bizarre phenomena and save their money.

A Ghostly Wagon and Combatants

The morning after they had voted in favor of frugality, a new manifestation occurred that may have been designed to make them reconsider their decision. At the first glimmer of dawn, the couples awakened to the sound of a heavy wagon creaking up the driveway. They could hear the unmistakable sound of shod hooves, jingling harnesses, and the murmur of men's voices. The phenomena, which culminated in an argument between two ghostly men, occurred at least twice a week thereafter.

When the three couples still gave no sign of moving, yet another disturbance was added to the repertoire of the haunting. Again, just before dawn, clanking sounds could be heard coming from an old rusted windmill at the rear of the house. There came the sound of a falling body that struck the metal structure on its way down, then came to rest with a heavy thud on the ground.

Mr. Murphy learned from some townspeople that a hired man had once fallen to his death from atop the windmill when a sudden gust of wind had swung the fan loose from its stabilizing brake. Apparently the three couples were being treated to an audio replay of the tragedy on alternating mornings with the creaking wagon and the argument.

The Panting Thing in the Basement

One of the husbands discovered yet another phenomenon when he went into the basement to get a jar of fruit. Something knocked him off a box as he stood on tiptoe, reaching for the highest shelf, then lay sighing in a dark corner of the fruit cellar. The other two men stopped laughing at their friend when they followed him back down into the basement and heard the thing sighing and panting like a giant bellows.

Mrs. Murphy's grandparents came for a visit, and Grandmother Woodruff, a tiny woman who possessed great psychic abilities, was quick to notice that there were "people" in the room with them. In spite of her husband's violent disapproval of such activity, she had gained a great reputation as a "rainmaker" and a levitator of furniture and household objects.

Grandmother Woodruff pointed to the portrait of the blond woman that hung above the fireplace and told the couples that the woman had been poisoned in one of the upstairs bedrooms. A frown from Grandfather Woodruff silenced her elaboration.

Later, when the others were gone, Mrs. Murphy asked her grandmother to attempt to gain additional psychic impressions. Grandmother Woodruff learned that something inhuman haunted the premises. "I'm not easily frightened," she said, "but whatever it is, I am terrified of it."

An Invisible Monster Attacks Grandmother Woodruff

Just as the elderly couple were preparing to leave, the invisible monster threw Grandmother Woodruff to the floor before the fireplace and began to choke her.

Grandmother's face was beginning to turn blue when her husband arrived to help her fight off the unseen foe. The thing slammed her to the floor when her husband called upon the name of God. Grandfather Woodruff managed to sweep his gasping wife into his arms and proclaimed the place a house of evil, advising the three couples to move at once.

Grandmother Woodruff, whose voice was now but a rasping whisper, said that she had been "talking" to the blond lady when she had seen an awful creature creep up behind her. "It was as big as a man but like nothing I've ever seen before. It had stiff, wiry orange hair standing out from its head. Its hands curved into talons. The arms were like a man's but covered with orange hair."

The beast had threatened to kill Grandmother Woodruff and had left cuts on her neck where its talons had gouged into her flesh. "I know that this house will burn down within a short time. Nothing will be left but the foundation," she warned her granddaughter.

The three couples decided to move a few days later after

a night during which a huge black bat had crept under the bedclothes and clamped its teeth into Mrs. Nelson's foot. It had taken two men to beat and pry the monstrous bat off her foot, and even after it had been clubbed to the floor it managed to rise, circle the room, and smash a window to escape.

Within a few weeks after the newlyweds left the mansion it burned to the ground.

The Murphy family's involvement with the hideous entity had not ended, however.

The Monster Moves With Them

Ten years after Grandmother Woodruff's death, several of her kin were living in her old ranch house in San Bernardino. Author Murphy's Uncle Jim came downstairs ashen-faced one night and said that he had seen an orange-haired "thing" poke its head out of the storage room, then shut the door. Although the family laughed at him, Uncle Jim later complained of "something" in his room at nights. The gales of derisive laughter ceased when Uncle Jim died.

In 1948, Murphy's parents decided to spend their vacation on Grandmother Woodruff's old ranch. For company they had the author's nine-year-old son, Mike, with them. Everything seemed comfortable in the old homestead on that first night until, at about three A.M., when Mrs. Murphy was awakened by something shuffling toward Mike.

According to Murphy: "Looking it full in the face, Mother saw a grinning mouth with huge, yellow teeth. Its eyes were almost hidden in a series of mottled lumps. . . . Brushing her aside, it lunged toward Mike, who was now wide awake. Mother grabbed a handful of its thick, long hair and desperately clutched a hairy, scaly arm with the other. In the moonlight she saw huge hands that curved into long talons. . . ."

By this time Mike was sitting up in bed screaming, watching helplessly as his grandmother did battle with the grotesque creature. At last Grandfather Murphy turned on the light in his room and came running to investigate the disturbance. The monster backed away from the light but continued to gesture toward Mike.

In the light Mrs. Murphy could see that the beast wore ". . . a light-colored, tight-fitting one-piece suit of a thin material which ended at knees and elbow." Bristly orange hair protruded from its flattened and grossly misshapen nose, and thick, bulbous lips drew back over snarling yellow teeth. It gestured again in Mike's direction, then turned and shuffled through the doorway, leaving behind a sickening odor of decay.

Whether the entity had been attracted to the young couples by the tensions of their marital adjustment, or whether it had been somehow activated by the vibrations of the life force emanating from their sexual activity, cannot be answered. Although the phenomena began with somewhat ordinary poltergeist disturbances, they seem to have culminated in either the creation, or the attraction of, a violent and malignant entity. To the Murphys, at least, it has been demonstrated that creatures haunting one's house can, if they will it, move their operations along with the family. The old ranch house, the entity's last habitat, was razed in 1952.

▪ 3 ▪

Haunted People

Recently one of my readers, Mrs. Helen Murad, now a fifty-two-year-old grandmother, sent me a lengthy bit of correspondence detailing an incident in her adolescence during which she swears she kissed a ghost!

When Helen was a teenager, she moved out into the country and left her friends back in the city. In those days school buses did not travel far beyond the city limits, and Helen found herself attending a country school. Every couple of weeks Helen's mother would take the children back to their hometown to obtain books at the library. Helen was completely removed from her old school friends, except for an occasional chance meeting in the quiet stacks of the library.

About a year after her family had moved to the country, Helen quickly selected the books she wished to check out, then sat on the library steps to await her mother's return.

"I had not sat there long," she recalled, "when I saw a familiar figure approaching me. It was Peter, a boy with whom I had gone to school a year before we moved. He was a handsome boy, and all of the girls always made such a fuss over him. He was a good athlete, too.

" 'Hey,' he said when he spotted me on the steps, 'it's

Helen. Boy, have you gotten prettier since you moved. Must be that country living!'

"I blushed and was putty in Peter's hands. I offered little resistance when he asked me to walk across the street to the park and sit on a bench with him. He put his arm around me, and even though my heart started thudding so hard that it hurt, I could take it. But I thought I would faint when he bent down and kissed me on the cheek!

"'I always liked you, Helen,' Peter said. 'I was sure sorry when you moved out to the country.'

"I told him that I had missed all the kids at first, but my new friends in the country school were nice, too.

"'Yeah, well, that's good,' Peter said, suddenly becoming rather glum. 'I'm going to go away, too.'

"My heart sank. I had just been creating the most beautiful mental pictures of Peter and me writing love letters back and forth and meeting when I came into town, and I even had a perfectly gorgeous image of seeing Peter drive down our lane in his old car. 'Where,' I asked reluctantly, 'are you moving?'

"'Far away, kid.' He sighed. 'Far, far away. You ain't never gonna see this old boy again!'

"I felt terribly depressed, and I thought for certain that I was going to cry.

"'How about another kiss?' Peter asked gently. 'A good-bye kiss.'

"This time Peter kissed me on the lips, and he held the kiss so long that I thought surely I would faint this time.

"When he finally let me go, I looked up into Mama's scowling face. She grabbed me by the hand, and I just barely had time to wave good-bye to Peter over my shoulder before Mama dragged me off to the car.

"I talked to Mama all the way home, trying to make her not be angry with me. When I explained that Peter was going to be moving away, she became somewhat more understanding and sympathetic, although she let me understand that she did not approve of any daughter of hers smooching on a bench in a public park."

It was nearly a month before Helen got back to the library. Illness and farm work had prevented her mother from taking the children into town any sooner, and they knew that the books would have overdue fines on them.

One of Helen's former classmates was working at the library desk, and as Helen doled out the fine she could not resist telling the girl how she and Peter had necked in the park a few weeks previously.

"That's bad taste, kid," the girl said, sniffing disdainfully. "Did you lose your class, moving out with the chickens and pigs?"

Helen frowned. "I suppose you would resist if Peter asked you to sit on a park bench with him. I can't remember you ever being such a goody-two-shoes."

"Wow!" the girl exclaimed, momentarily forgetting about the large QUIET! sign over her head. "You must be getting goofy sitting out there on that farm. Goofy or just plain crude!"

The head librarian came to shush the girls, and Helen's former classmate turned to walk away from her.

"Don't go!" Helen whispered sharply, catching her friend's arm. "We always got along so well. Why do you accuse me of bad taste and call me goofy because I let Peter kiss me? Is it just jealousy or what?"

Her friend fixed Helen with a cold stare. Then something within Helen's own eyes caused the girl to thaw just a bit. "Look, Helen," she began, "every girl daydreams once in a while, and I suppose we all tell fibs to our friends now and then, but I think it was in bad taste for you to say that Peter kissed you a couple of weeks ago. Say it was any other boy but Peter."

Helen shook her head. "It wasn't a fib. Peter did kiss me. And what's wrong with Peter? You know he's the dreamiest boy in the class."

Tears began to form in her friend's eyes. "I don't know if you are serious or not," she told Helen. "If you're just being crude, then I really feel sorry for you, Helen." The girl took a deep breath and continued. "Peter *was* the dreamiest boy in our class. He was killed in an automobile accident shortly after you moved away."

Helen could find no words to utter as she watched the back of her friend moving away from her. *Peter dead!* It simply could not be. She recognized another former classmate across the library and nearly ran to the table where the girl sat flipping through a magazine. She confirmed the startling news of Peter's death.

Helen Murad can provide no explanation of the experience she had with that affectionate ghost over thirty years ago. But, she emphasizes, she knows that she sat on that park bench and received a warm kiss from a boy who had been dead for over a year, and she can offer the additional testimony of her mother, who saw Peter as unmistakably as Helen had.

A Jealous Ghost in Kiel, Germany

In Kiel in northwest Germany in the early 1920s, a case of what appeared to be a jealous ghost was well documented by the police, a number of university professors, and several psychic investigators.

Shortly after World War I a laundryman married a woman

who had had a child by a sailor who had gone down in the Battle of Jutland. The first few months of the marriage were uneventful. Then, one morning when the husband sat down to his breakfast, a scalding cup of hot coffee leapt from the table and tossed its steaming contents in his face.

While the man reached in agony for a napkin with which to sop up the liquid, assorted pieces of crockery and cutlery became animated and began to hop up and down on the table like popcorn on a griddle. As he shouted for his wife to come witness the phenomena, the lively saucers, knives, and spoons began to launch themselves at his head. Unfortunately he was unable to duck all of the suddenly hostile missiles from his breakfast table.

The laundryman staggered off his chair, bruised by a blow to his temple, and his chair shot to the ceiling and smashed itself to pieces.

An Exploding Bed

Act two of the eerie drama took place one night when the man attempted the natural act of getting into bed with his wife. He threw back the blankets, reached out his arms to embrace his wife, and the headboard split with a startlingly loud crack just inches from his ear. Before the astonished man could swing his legs out of bed, the mattress suddenly decided to emulate a magic carpet. The mattress elevated both itself and the wide-eyed couple for several inches, then dumped them onto the floor.

The husband and wife were given no time to sputter their thoughts as to the nature of the unearthly disturbance that had beset them. A large clothing cabinet toppled forward onto them, and the husband was barely able to get an arm up in time to prevent the heavy piece of furniture from crashing painfully against their skulls.

He maneuvered to his knees and began to push the cabinet back to its original standing position. He nearly lost control of the piece when he heard his wife screaming. Turning his back to see what invisible monster had attacked from the rear, he was terrified to discover that the blankets on their bed were being consumed by crackling flames.

Vicious Rampages

The couple decided that they had moved into a haunted house, but it soon became apparent that the increasingly vicious rampages were directed only against the husband. Whenever he entered a room, whatever object was closest to him would launch a direct frontal attack against his head. If he managed to sneak into a room seemingly undetected, the chair on which he sat would be jerked out from under him, and if he did not move fast enough, it would be cracked against his skull. On several occasions, drawers the man had opened flamed up in spontaneous combustion.

The man and wife moved to a hotel, only to have their room become almost immediately transformed into an aggressively animated nightmare of wildly dancing furniture. They were forced to move from one hotel to another, then to a succession of rooming houses as the phenomena and angered room managers evicted them from room after room.

Anyone who tried to investigate the mysterious plague found himself beset with similar woes. Policemen, professors, and psychic researchers had their clothes burst into flame or torn from their bodies. More than one officer was struck by some unseen aggressor. In one instance a police car on the way to investigate the reported disturbances suffered three flat tires and two collisions within a mile.

The Ghost of a Jealous Sailor

At last one psychic investigator brought with him a medium of high repute. In her entranced state the medium told the couple and the assembled witnesses that the jealous spirit of the sailor who had been killed in action was responsible for the violent maelstrom of psychic activity. Since the medium had in some way received the impressions of the deceased sailor, and the fact that the sailor, rather than the laundryman, was the father of the couple's child, it seemed to follow that her conclusion that the sailor's spirit was the couple's unseen tormentor was also correct.

The denouement of the case came when the laundryman and his bride of a few months agreed to separate in order to save his life. Whether by an actual statement from the medium or by their own assessment of her entranced relay of information, the newlyweds had inferred that the sailor's jealous spirit would not rest until it had killed the unsurper of his woman's affections.

Bigotry Died at Graveside

Carol G. knew that because of religious reasons, her grandfather did not approve of Jack S. courting her. Grandpa G. had strong convictions that one should marry within one's faith, and it may have been the psychological tension her grandfather created within her unconscious that led to a flurry of poltergeist activity around the teenage girl.

For a period of nearly two weeks Jack's visits to the house were accompanied by violent outbursts of psychokinetic energy. Mrs. G's favorite vase shattered as the two young people held hands on the sofa. Invisible hands banged on the piano keyboard, and the piano stool jumped across the living-room floor and struck Carol smartly across the shins.

One night as the young lovers had just finished making a tray of cookies and were allowing them to cool, the entire two dozen smoldered into flames. As in most poltergeist attacks, the unconscious energy center of the disturbance received the brunt of its abuse and physical torment. Stigmatalike scratches appeared on Carol's upper arms, and on one occasion teeth marks appeared just below her shoulder blades.

"You're to blame for this," Grandpa G. said one night, advancing upon Jack with his cane. "To mix religions is to do the devil's work, and you've brought the devil upon us."

The old man swung his cane and caught Jack stoutly across the forehead. Jack jumped to his feet, dazed and angry, but was restrained by his sweetheart. "If you were thirty years younger . . ." Jack said, grimly clenching his fists.

The poltergeist activity eventually spent its psychic energy, and the vortex of paranormal disturbances subsided.

In spite of Grandpa G's fulminations, Carol's parents were open-minded toward a religiously mixed marriage and gave their consent for the young people to be wed.

Grandpa G. contracted pneumonia a month before the wedding date and passed away in an oxygen tent in the hospital. In spite of their differences over religion and her choice of a husband, Carol was genuinely sorrowful when the old man died.

A few psychic strands of unconscious guilt over marrying outside her religious faith and against her grandfather's wishes may have set in motion the bizarre phenomena that visited Carol on her wedding night, but the manifestations had a most positive conclusion.

The newlyweds had checked into the nearest motel, eager to consummate their marriage. They had no sooner gone to bed, however, than they were sharply distracted by a loud knocking on the wall beside them.

The honeymooners tried desperately to ignore the sound and blamed it on a noisy party next door, but the more they listened to the rapping, the more they both realized that it sounded very much like Grandpa's cane. Their passion was replaced by apprehension.

As they watched in amazement, a glowing orb of light appeared beside their bed. As the illumination grew larger and took shape, they were astonished to see a wispy outline of Carol's grandfather standing before them.

"He . . . he's smiling," Carol said, somehow managing to force words past her fear and surprise.

As the young couple lay in each other's arms they saw the image of Grandpa G. smile, then move his cane in the sign of the cross, and then in a gesture of farewell.

"He's blessed us, Jack," Carol said, tears welling in her eyes as she watched the ethereal form of her grandfather fade away. "He understands now that he's on the other side. Earthly differences don't matter over there."

• 4 •

Entities That Seek to Possess and Destroy

The skeptics say with finality that the evil thoughts and emotions of the living or the dead cannot overpower the healthy brain of a normal person. The mind cannot be subdued unless by physical distortion or disease.

There are intelligent men and women who feel otherwise. They are convinced that they have felt the touch of demons. In their experience the admonition "Get thee behind me, Satan" is by no means a fanciful directive.

Serious individuals claim to have undergone fearsome ordeals in which either they or their loved ones became the targets of vile entities that sought the possession of physical bodies and minds in order that they might enjoy the sensations of demonically aroused mortals who yield to ungodly temptations.

Skeptics will dismiss such stories as examples of psychological disorders, but certain psychic researchers—as well as those who have been victimized—argue that demonic possession is not insanity, for in most cases the possession is only temporary. The individual who has become possessed is unable to control himself, although he may be entirely conscious of the fiendish manipulation of his mind and body, and in many instances may actually see grotesque, devilish faces before him.

A Saintly Woman Possessed by a Vulgar Spirit

Caroline Spencer is a nurse who specializes in private care. A few years ago she received a job offer from a young businessman whose wife had become crippled in a hunting accident. The couple had no children, and the wife was lonely, as well as in need of professional care.

"My wife is an absolute saint," the man told Miss Spencer over the telephone. "She never complains."

When Miss Spencer arrived at their residence, the husband had already left on a three-day business trip. She let herself in with the key that had been sent to her, and she found the woman, Mrs. Eston, in her bedroom.

"Hello, Caroline, baby," the woman greeted her, a strange smile stretching her lips in a leer. "Oh, my, we are going to get along just fine."

Miss Spencer was surprised at the display of familiarity upon their first meeting. She asked Mrs. Eston how she had learned her first name, and the woman told her that she knew lots of things about Caroline.

"Her eyes had a strange cast to them," Miss Spencer said in her report. "There almost seemed to be a flame flickering behind each of them."

Miss Spencer put in an exhausting first night. Every few minutes Mrs. Eston would summon her to her bedside on some pretext, then complain loudly about the nurse's general incompetence.

When Miss Spencer suggested that they should both get

some sleep, Mrs. Eston laughed and said, "I don't need to sleep. And you, my dear, are not going to get *any*!"

The next morning Mrs. Eston mocked her by telling her how tired and worn-out she looked. "You could use a beauty nap, my dear."

Miss Spencer could not wait to meet Mr. Eston in person and let him have a piece of her mind. So his wife was a saint and never complained?

She decided to call Mrs. Eston's doctor and arrange for some tranquilizers for the woman so she could get some rest. When the nurse explained the problem to the doctor, he expressed his amazement and said that he would stop by on his way home.

An Obscene Entity

The nurse had no sooner hung up the phone when she heard a deep male voice singing an obscene song. Miss Spencer put a weary hand to her throbbing forehead. The voice was coming from Mrs. Eston's room. Had the "saint" taken herself a coarse lover to while away the long hours in bed? Although the accident had crippled her, she remained a breathtakingly attractive woman, although a bit emaciated.

"For a moment I though I was losing my mind," Miss Spencer said. "The deep, foul voice was coming from Mrs. Eston's own throat."

"So you called the doctor, huh?" the voice said grimly. "You're a tattletale, honey, but you are going to be in for a surprise."

When the doctor arrived, Mrs. Eston was completely composed, and she spoke in cultured, well-modulated tones. She was sweet, pleasant, the very picture of the long-suffering, ideal patient.

GHOSTS AMONG US

The doctor stopped for a cup of coffee with Caroline before he left. He tried to make the conversation about medical schools and courses of study sound casual and shoptalkish, but Caroline knew that he was sounding her out about her background. Behind his pleasant, professional smile he was questioning her qualifications as a private nurse.

Before he left, he told Caroline that he could see no reason to prescribe tranquilizers for Mrs. Eston and, in his brusque manner, suggested that she could benefit more than Mrs. Eston from such a prescription.

As soon as the doctor had gone, the deep voice began howling with laughter and delivered foul curses at Miss Spencer. The nurse walked back to the bedroom, looked deep into the black, glittering eyes. "Why do you do such things, Mrs. Eston?" was all she could manage, and the strange woman mocked her for her weakness.

A Physical Attack

For two nights Miss Spencer bore the curses and imprecations of the deep voice that boomed from within the frail, crippled woman.

Once, when the nurse was attempting to bathe her, Mrs. Eston's hand shot out to grasp her by the throat. Miss Spencer nearly blacked out before she managed to wrest the powerful fingers from her throat.

"You're a strong woman," the deep voice said approvingly as the nurse sat gasping on the floor. "How are you in bed, honey? Can you show a man a good time? If I could get these legs working, I would sure as hell find out."

Miss Spencer looked up in horror at the black eyes, looking down on her with such evil appraisal. Dimly, in the back of her mind, strange thoughts were beginning to collect, thoughts long ago banished by her scientific training.

"You beginning to get the picture now, honey?" the voice asked. "Mrs. Eston, hell! You come close to me again and you'll find out who I really am!"

A Brief Period of Peace

That night the foul voice stopped shouting selections from what seemed to be an inexhaustible supply of filth. Miss Spencer could hear the sound of soft crying coming from Mrs. Eston's room. When she investigated, she found the woman lying in a state of confusion.

"Who are you?" Mrs. Eston demanded in a weak voice. "Where's my husband? What's happening to me? Oh, nurse, whoever you are, please keep that ugly brute away from me!"

Miss Spencer fed Mrs. Eston some soup and took advantage of the lull to bathe her. She talked soothingly to the woman, and when she had left Mrs. Eston so that they both might get some rest, she allowed the terrible thought to escape from the corner of her brain where she had kept it chained: *Mrs. Eston was possessed.*

If Miss Spencer had hoped for sleep that night, there was none to be had. She had just lain down to rest when she heard Mrs. Eston vomiting.

"No food for you, bitch!" roared the deep voice over and over again in between the sounds of the woman retching. "And no rest for you until I stop your heart!"

Miss Spencer ran to the woman with cold cloths, but she was given no opportunity to clean the mess. "Let her lie in filth and vomit," the angry voice warned her. "Let the bitch die. You come closer and I'll wring your silly neck!"

Calling on the Name of God

"No," Miss Spencer said. "I know what you are now. With God's help I'll do my duty."

The nurse spoke of God's love and of how God answered prayers. The thing that had invaded Mrs. Eston clamped palms to her ears and screamed that it would not listen to such talk. While it was thus distracted, Miss Spencer cleaned up the vomit that had spewed out of the woman.

When Mr. Eston returned the next day, Miss Spencer's haggard appearance told him that his worst fears had been realized. He begged the nurse's forgiveness. "I thought . . . I hoped she might be different for you," he said by way of explanation.

At Miss Spencer's prompting, Mr. Eston told of how they had found his wife's body lying inside an old stone hut on the day of the hunting accident. No one could ever understand why she had gone into the hut or how she had accidentally shot herself. The only theory they had developed was that she had set her shotgun against a wall and it has slipped off the moist rock and gone off when it had struck the floor. The pellets had damaged her spine and had rendered her paralyzed from the waist down.

The nature of the hut? Nothing special, just an old house where some nutty old recluse had lived and died, hating mankind.

"And now," Mr. Eston said, fighting to hold back tears, "my poor wife has been transformed into some kind of incredible lunatic. How that deep voice comes out of her, I'll never understand."

A Physical Victory for the Dark Side

At almost the same instant Miss Spencer and Mr. Eston realized that it had become silent in his wife's room. "Let me check," the nurse told the anxious husband.

"I shall never forget that sight," Miss Spencer wrote. "I have seen death in many manifestations, but I know I shall never see the equal of what I saw in that room. Mrs. Eston's facial features were distorted into an expression of malignant evil. The face lying on that pillow resembled that of a gargoyle or some hideous demon. Somehow I managed to check for pulse and respiration. There was none. I returned to Mr. Eston and told him that he should not enter the bedroom. He would never have recognized the features of his once-beautiful wife.

"Later I learned that Mrs. Eston had been buried quietly, closed casket. The mortician had worked for several hours on her face, but her features continued to slip back into that horrible grimace. Whatever had possessed Mrs. Eston had won a physical victory. I only pray that it had not been able to claim the woman's soul as well as her body."

The Possession of Yvonne Marchand

Author Ed Bodin tells of the possession of beautiful Yvonne Marchand, the daughter of Colonel Marchand, the French officer who had been sent to take command of the French detachment in Indochina in 1923. The lovely, blond eighteen-year old had become the belle of the military colony, and Colonel Marchand's troubles seemed few. Although he was of the old military school and contemptuous of native beliefs, the natives, for the most part, tolerated him.

The Accursed Swamp

The colonel's principal error in public relations lay in the area of what he thought was natives trespassing on military property. A native corporal explained to the officer that the reason for such regular trespassing could be found in the people's desire to avoid going through a certain demon-possessed swamp to get to the hills beyond. According to native legend, he who passed through the swamp at night would become possessed of fiendish demons. Colonel Marchand found only amusement in such an account.

One day a native thief surrendered, rather than seek escape by running into the accursed swamp. Colonel Marchand decided to demonstrate the qualities of French mercy, so rather than having the man shot, he ordered him cast into the midst of the swamp, so that the thief would have to wade through the area he so feared.

The felon begged the colonel to reconsider, and he attempted to throw himself at the feet of the colonel's daughter to beseech her understanding. All he accomplished, unfortunately, was to trip Yvonne. In a rage, the officer had the man forced into the swamp at bayonet point.

That night Yvonne's maid rushed to the colonel with the news of the thief's terrible revenge. He had managed to creep back into camp and carried off the colonel's daughter. A search was immediately organized, but the native corporal feared the worst when the trail led to the swamp.

A solider met the search party at the edge of the swamp.

The thief had been found bleeding to death, his face and body covered with scratches, his jugular vein torn open. With his dying words he had gasped that the beautiful Yvonne had wrenched herself free of his grasp and had turned on him with her teeth and nails.

The men searched an hour with powerful spotlights and lanterns before they caught sight of something white moving ahead of them in the swamp. It was Yvonne, naked except for strips of cloth around her thighs.

The searchlight caught the streaks of blood on her body, but her father was most horrified by her face. A fiendish grin parted her lips, and her teeth flashed as if she were some wild thing waiting for prey to fall within reach of claw and fang. She rushed the nearest solider, ready to gouge and bite.

Colonel Marchand ran to his daughter's side. She eluded his grasp, seemed about to turn on him, then collapsed at his feet. Her shoulders and breasts were covered with the indentations of dozens of teeth marks. The colonel covered his daughter's nakedness from the curious gaze of the soldiers and called for a litter on which to have Yvonne carried home.

Horrible Laughing Faces

Later, when the girl regained consciousness, she told a most frightening and bizarre story. The thief had clamped a hand over her mouth and dragged her into the swamp. When he had stopped to rest, Yvonne had become aware of horrible faces bobbing all around them.

"A terrible sensation came over me," the girl said. "Never before have I felt anything like it. I wanted only to kill the man, to bite his throat, to tear at his face. I have never had such strength before. I mangled him as if he were a child. I gloried in ripping his flesh, in seeing him drop to the ground and crawl away. Then the faces summoned me on into the swamp. I tore off my clothes and began to bite myself. The faces laughed at me, and I laughed too."

When Yvonne had seen the searchers' lights, she became angry and had wanted to kill them. "And, Father," she went on, "I knew you, but I wanted to kill you, too. I kept trying to think of you as my father, but something kept tearing at my brain. Then, when you reached out to touch me, the awful fire that was burning inside me seemed to fall away."

Thereafter Colonel Marchund was much more sympathetic to the hill people who trespassed across a small portion of the military property to avoid the swamp. His daughter had said over and over again that if there truly were a hell, that swamp must be it.

Eventually the swamp was completely filled in by earth and stone from a more godly spot of ground. Yvonne Marchand bore no lasting ill effects from her ordeal and later married and produced healthy children. But when friends got her to tell of her night of possession in the Indochinese swamp, few walked away as skeptics.

The Man Who Runs A Sanctuary For Earthbound Spirits

It was just after dark when medium Donald Page and Reverend John D. Pearce-Higgins, an eminent canon of the Church of England, arrived at the house in Stoke Newington, England, where a disagreeable ghost had been annoying and frightening women.

"The ghost was a most distressed thing," the medium

recalled. "He was the spirit of a cobbler who had passed from the earth plane about eighty years ago. He had been an ugly, stooped-over dwarf despised by women. Because he had been humiliated by women so often when he was alive, he had decided to stick around his old shop after death and take his revenge on women by frightening them half to death."

The ghost-hunting duo soon learned that the haunted house had been constructed on the site of the cobbler's old shop.

"No wonder he has been so angry toward you," Page explained to the terrified lady of the house.

But once Page was in a trance, he found himself possessed by the spirit of the woman-hating cobbler, and the vengeance-seeking spirit did not go for the lady of the house but for the throat of the medium's assistant, Mrs. Edna Taylor.

"It was most fortunate that Canon Pearce-Higgins was there to pull me off Mrs. Taylor," Page said later.

"The spirit was utilizing my body the way one would pull the strings of a puppet, and I had no control over my own person," the medium explained. "Eventually the canon managed to tranquilize the spirit of the cobbler, and we brought the ghost to my sanctuary, where my spirit guides could help him on his way."

In the spring of 1969, Donald Page told reporter Peter Thompson that he had been running a home for wayward ghosts for nearly three years. Page, who has been a medium since he was fifteen, freely admitted that he kept a spare bedroom in his London apartment expressly for the purpose of offering shelter and spiritual comfort to the ghosts he had dispossessed from their old haunts—where their presence had been decidedly unwelcome by the human occupants.

The small guest room, decorated with psychic artwork,

affords the displaced spirit an opportunity to adjust to life in a transitional state before it moves on to a higher, more spiritual plane of existence.

Page explained that entities who used his guest room were ". . . evil earthbound spirits who have been bothering people."

Assisting Evil Earthbound Entities to Move On

The medium emphasized the point that one could not simply remove such spirits from the places they haunt and leave them to flounder helplessly in a spiritual twilight zone.

"These spirits must be helped out of their earthbound state and assisted in continuing their journey to paradise," Page said. "The ghost sanctuary is essential in this respect."

Page went on to state that they permit the ghosts to stay in the sanctuary until they have regained their spiritual equilibrium and feel like moving on to the next plane of existence. Canon Pearce-Higgins, together with Page's spirit guides, conditioned the spirits for the journey from the earth state into the astral plane, then ". . . into the etheric state, in which the spirits will find peace and contentment."

Medium Page and clergyman Pearce-Higgins have been a ghost-hunting team for more than fifteen years, and they claim to have helped hundreds of ghosts find peace.

"Why, in the two and a half years that I've kept the guest room in my present apartment," Page declared, "we've extended hospitality to three hundred spirits."

Canon Pearce-Higgins keeps a well-documented account of the ghost-hunting team's experiences for the Church of England's Fellowship for Psychical Research. The cleric has stated that their primary aim is to help both the haunters and the haunted, and that they take their work very seriously. When the two men aren't busy helping restless spirits to move along to higher realms, Reverend Pearce-Higgins is minister of London's Southwark Cathedral; and Page heads a Spiritualist church, the Fellowship and Brotherhood of Paul.

When they receive a request from someone who is experiencing an unpleasant haunting, the "ghost squad" goes into immediate action. If investigation reveals that the haunting is being caused by a troubled ghost, Page goes into a trance and permits the spirit to possess him.

"That's the point where my guides take over," Page told Thompson. "It's up to them to remove the spirit from me. Then my spirit guides take the troubled spirit to my sanctuary. The ghosts get to my apartment long before we do, of course."

The spiritual ministers keep their ailing ghosts in the sanctuary for as long as it takes to assist them through the transitional period. During this time of spiritual therapy the two men and their assistant, Mrs. Taylor, are able to keep the troubled spirits in a happier frame of mind, and with the help of Page's spirit guides, they show the confused ghosts the way to continue their journey to the other side.

In May of 1971, Donald Page told writer John Dodd that as of that date his personal tally of ghosts helped along was around five hundred. By now, the medium told the journalist, the ghost-relief team had developed a routine. Canon John Pearce-Higgins held a short requiem Mass, then Page slipped into a trance and made contact with his spirit guide to allow a ghost to speak.

Canon Pearce-Higgins said that in his estimation the Spiritualist philosophy of death explained ". . . the New Testament, the Resurrection, the 'many mansions' of God's house, the miracles. I want to see the established churches acknowledging these principles."

The Canon admitted that many people might doubt the efficacy and the validity of their work, but ". . . all I know is that when we go into a house and do our stuff and the phenomena stop, we assume it is because of what we have done."

· 5 ·

Phantoms of Fields, Forests, and Shores

As a reporter of the strange and the unknown, I am always appreciative of accounts of eerie encounters with ghosts that are passed on to me by those who have read my books and magazine articles. Here is one such account. The names are altered to protect the right to privacy.

Mary was ten years old at the time of the incident, eighty-three when she told this tale, but as she remarked, "There are some experiences that a body just doesn't forget."

Mary and her family were sitting around a fire one bitter winter night, and her mother began to talk of William, the oldest son, who had sailed with the fishing fleets. "It has been so long since we heard from him," the mother complained.

"You know how fishermen are about writing," the younger brother said, trying to make light of her maternal concern.

But that night during their prayers, the anxious mother insisted that they have a special prayer for William.

Later Mary remembers being awakened by her mother, who said that she heard the sounds of oars moving upon the ocean. Since the family lived in a fishing village, they could not understand why these oars should be of special concern to their mother.

"At her insistence," Mary recalled, "I opened the window and listened to the sounds of the oars dipping into the sea. I also heard the unmistakable sound of male voices, but I could not make out what was being said."

"Maybe they're in some kind of trouble," Mother remarked. "Mary, light a lantern and hang it outside. Let us do what we can to guide those poor men to shore."

Mary did as she was told, but she could not see a boat offshore, and no knock came on their door that night from fishermen seeking shelter.

The next day Mother made inquiries of coast guardsmen regarding the possibility of any lost boats, but all replies were negative.

"Mother returned to the house pale and drawn," Mary said. "She seemed to sense in the sound of the oarsmen some significance that escaped the rest of us."

The evening meal was not made easier when Peter, the younger brother, complained of his sisters' careless handling of fresh meat.

"Look!" he growled. "Someone has sprinkled blood on the back of my hand."

Since no fresh meat had been prepared that evening, Mother regarded the mysterious appearance of the droplets of blood to be a grim omen concerning William's fate.

"That night," Mary remembered, "we had no sooner shut out the lights when we heard the splash of oars, two and two alternately striking the water. I got up as I had the night before, the lantern in my hand.

"I stood on the beach and saw nothing but a clear stretch of ocean. No boat was to be seen, yet the 'plish-plish' of oars sounded on as monotonously and distinctly as the regular ticking of a metronome.

"Peter joined me on the beach, but his more experienced eyes could no more sight a boat than could my own."

When the two rejoined their mother and younger sister in the seaside cottage, Peter, in answer to Mother's question, replied that perhaps she was correct. Maybe they were receiving a "fisherman's warning" about William.

"Two nights later, when the fishing fleet returned," Mary said, "we were given the sad news over the canvas-wrapped corpse of our older brother. On the evening during which we had first heard the sound of the phantom oarsmen, William had slipped over the side of the boat and had drowned in the heavy waves before he could be rescued."

The Girl Ghost of White Rock Lake

Texans who live near White Rock Lake have reported the nocturnal prowlings of an apparition; it is that of a girl in a dripping wet evening gown who appears on the lakeshore.

Young couples, who have parked beside the lake to take full advantage of the bright moon reflecting on the placid waters, have told some hair-raising tales about the phantom. One young man said that he would never forget the sight of the shimmering ghost looking in the car window at him and his frightened date.

Frank X. Tolbert, columnist for the *Dallas Morning News*, dealt with the legend of the alleged girl ghost and received hundreds of letters and phone calls in response to his article. Apparently the apparition had been seen and firmly attested to by a good number of people.

Mr. Dale Berry told Tolbert that he and his family had purchased a home near White Rock Lake in September 1962. On their first night in their new home Berry hurried to the door to answer the ringing of the bell. There was no one there. The bell rang a second time. In spite of a rapid dash to the door, whoever had rung the bell had vanished.

The third time the bell rang, Berry's daughter answered the door. Soon the entire family was clustered around the front door in response to the girl's screams. There, on the porch, were large puddles of water, as if someone dripping wet had stood there. There were large droplets of water on the steps and the walk leading up to the front door, yet the sprinkler system had not been turned on, the rest of the yard was dry, and the night was clear and cloudless. Moreover, the neighbors were not the sort to indulge in practical jokes.

It appeared that the Girl Ghost of White Rock Lake had been trying to pay the newcomers a visit to welcome them.

The Phantom Sioux Warrior Who Races Trains

A traveling salesman was making the night trip from Minneapolis, Minnesota, to Butte, Montana. He had been dozing lightly in a lower berth when he was awakened by what he later described as a "damned uneasy feeling."

"I couldn't put my finger on what was troubling me," he told a reporter for a Chicago newspaper in the summer of 1943. "There were no strange or unusual noises in the train. I could detect nothing that sounded wrong in the steady clicking of the wheels. For some reason I decided to lift my window shade."

That was when he saw the apparition. Outside of his window, so close that it seemed as if he might be able to touch them if he lowered the glass, was a brightly painted Indian brave on his spirited mount. The warrior bent low over the flying black mane of his horse and looked neither to the right nor to the left. He seemed to be mouthing words of encouragement to the phantom mustang as they rapidly gained on the train.

"I've seen them five or six times after that, in different parts of the Dakotas," the salesman said. "They seem to be solid flesh, but there's a kind of shimmering around them. It's like watching a strip of really old movie film being projected onto the prairie."

Railroad brakemen, engineers, and construction crews in the Dakotas and Wyoming have often spoken of the phantom Sioux and his determined race with their swift, modern iron horses.

"They couldn't beat the trains when they were alive," said one old-timer, who knew the legend behind the spectral racers, "but they seem to have picked up some speed in the happy hunting grounds."

Frederic Remington, the famous artist of the Old West, sketched the Sioux brave and his mustang from life as the inexhaustible pair raced the train on which he was riding. Remington had heard from several travelers the same tale, of a determined warrior astride a big, bony mustang who tirelessly raced the trains as the iron horses steamed across the plains. It was as if the locomotive represented a tangible symbol of the encroaching white man, and the Sioux believed that if he could conquer the iron horses, his people could vanquish the paleface invaders.

With a marrow-chilling war whoop the warrior would come astride the train engines as they entered a wide-open stretch of the prairie. The mustang would pound the plains until sweat formed on its lean, hard body. Only the greater speed of the locomotives would at last enable them to pull away from the chanting Sioux and his indefatigable mount. Even in life the two had seemed more phantom than flesh.

One can easily sense the great admiration Remington had

for the spirit of the Sioux and his animal as his sensitive hands recreated the intensity of its master. Remington named his sketch "America on the Move."

The Devil Rider of Chisholm Hollow

The first settlers of the central Texas hill country were Scotch-Irish hillmen who had migrated from the states of Kentucky and Tennessee. God-fearing though they were, a vein of superstition and a healthy respect for the supernatural ran through their heritage. When advised by the Indians to avoid a small valley because of a strange apparition that appeared on horseback, they told themselves there was enough land to go around without trespassing on haunted ground, and steered wide of the foreboding little hollow.

Mysterious sounds, like metal striking metal, came from the hollow and were heard by the Indians and the few white men who dared get near enough the place to hear anything; but most reasonable folk had written off the reports as tall tales.

One of the "reasonable" people who had done so was a rancher named McConnell. A maurauding pack of wolves had been tearing at his herd, and he had tracked them to the draw that led into the hollow. Without hesitation he pushed on into the little valley over ground that had seldom supported the weight of a human being. After going a hundred yards he dismounted his horse and bent over to examine more closely the array of animal tracks.

The clank of metal and the sound of hooves caused him to snap up his head. He was astounded to see an armored rider thundering down the hollow. Terrified, he jumped on his own pony and galloped out of the place toward his house.

Shortly after the incident the people of the hill country learned that the army of General Zachary Taylor had crossed the Rio Grande and had violated Mexican territory. The Mexican War had begun.

The Devil Rider of Chisholm Hollow is a strange manifestation that the people of the central Texas hills have seen before every major conflict in which the United States has become embroiled. The strikingly tall armored horseman—on his magnificent, coal-black steed—is seen to thunder out of the little valley, then vanish without a trace.

Omen of the Civil War

The second recorded appearance of the rider was fifteen years after he had terrified McConnell. The report was given by Emmett Ringstaff, and this time the Devil Rider was more completely described.

On April 10, 1861, Ringstaff happened to be passing the hollow when the rider came by him at a steady trot. The horse he rode was taller than any raised by the settlers of the area, and even though the hill folk thought the rider to be a manifestation of Lucifer, Ringstaff remained calm enough to observe that the specter was wearing some kind of armor and carrying a shield. Iron gauntlets covered his arms, and he wore a helmet of Spanish design. Two brass pistols dangled from a buckler, that looked to be gold and bore symbols of a crown and a lion. The pistols were of eighteenth-century design and had the look of fine craftsmanship about them. Shortly after Ringstaff had seen the apparition, the first guns of the Civil War were fired at Fort Sumter.

After the war ended, the hollow was christened Chisholm

Hollow because of its geographical location on a spur of the Chisholm Trail, which Texas cattle owners used to drive their stock to Kansas railheads. Though the rider never seemed to bother the cattlemen, the cowboys did happen to pick up out of the hollow a few interesting articles, including a large silver spur that was Spanish in origin.

Still later, the settlers learned from historians that a Spanish fort had been located near the hollow when Texas had been under Spain's control. According to the historians, the garrison that had been stationed near the fort had been massacred by Comanche Indians around 1700.

Presage of the Spanish-American War

Gradually the theory that the rider was a manifestation of the devil gave way to the notion that he was the shade of one of the Spaniards who had been killed in the massacre two centuries before.

Before the Spanish-American War, the mysterious rider was seen by three men—Arch Clawson, Ed Shannon, and Sam Bulluck. Although the pattern of his visitation had not changed, a new twist had been added. Each one of the men who saw the rider felt, at that particular instant, a weird flash of personal animosity, which the rider seemed to have directed at him. Was the shade sensitive about his Spanish heritage?

Though the strange horseman had remained neutral when portending other conflicts, this time his loyalty lay with Spain, and it seemed to be showing. During the brief conflict with the European power, strange things happened around the central Texas hills. Though Texas had better than average rainfall in 1898, wells and creeks went dry in the hill country. Cattle died of thirst, and a strange and unexplainable disease began taking the horses. The calamity is still blamed on the Devil Rider by locals who live near the hollow.

Only one attempt was ever made to settle the hollow, and that was unsuccessful. Scoffing at the superstitions of the small ranching community, the settler began building a house so he could claim his homestead right on the land in the hollow. He had just completed the structure when the entire building seemed to erupt in flames. All that has remained is a crumbling chimney—the Devil Rider's hollow still remains unmolested.

The Devil Rider Announces World War I

After its appearance before the Spanish-American War, the apparition kept to itself in the secluded hollow. His next visitation was made in January 1917, to a group of young deer hunters who were tempting the fates by looking for deer sign within the hollow.

Laughing at the wild tales of their elders but glancing over their shoulders just the same, they entered the hollow very cautiously. When the armored rider thundered out of nowhere, his armor and mail glinting in the January sun, the young men scattered and ran. On February 3, 1917, the United States, which had been teetering on the brink of war, severed diplomatic relations with the German Empire and shortly after was sending armies across the Atlantic.

. . . And World War II

The world was hypertense in 1941. Europe had been a battlefield for over a year and a half, and the Western Pacific had been subject to Japanese aggression for even longer. Not insensitive to the precarious position of the United States in this world setting, the people of the central hills of Texas had gathered to pray for peace on Sunday, December 7, 1941.

Following the services, a group of settlers got into an automobile and started down the road that led to Chisholm Hollow. As the driver passed the haunted chasm, he stopped the car, claiming he had heard a horse. After a few seconds the mounted apparition charged onto the road, stopped broadside them for an instant, then passed off the road, and disappeared in the cover of trees on the opposite side.

The terrified group of men and women hurried home where they waited impatiently around the radio as the tubes warmed up. The first word they heard was of the bombing of Pearl Harbor.

Although the Devil Rider was not seen prior to the "police actions" of Korea and Vietnam, some doom-sayers have speculated that the spirit waits to bring on Armageddon.

The Headless Phantom of Oklahoma

Today great planes fly over the old trails where the covered wagons once lumbered into the sunset, and the super expresses roar past the oil wells and the slush tanks that fringe the Chicago, Rock Island, and Pacific Railroad, but superimposed on these modern settings are the shadows and phantoms of people and things that linger on for those who are sensitive to their vibrations.

Come with me to a cave not far from the North Fork of the Red River. In the early 1890s the territory thereabout, which once belonged to the Cheyenne and the Arapaho Indians, was opened for settlement. About that time an old trapper, known as Uncle Billie Morse, discovered a cave frequented by raccoons, or coons as they were more generally known locally. Outside of the cave he observed a number of watermelon vines, which apparently had been cultivated at a much earlier date. He called the place Coon Cave, and the name clings today.

Sometime later, settlers chased a coyote that had run into the cave. Determined to catch it, they armed themselves with lanterns and nets and entered the cave, which was much larger than they had anticipated, since Uncle Billie had not troubled to explore it to any extent. The roof lowered some fifty feet from the mouth, and the men had to crawl. A short, narrow passage led into an inner cave.

The Skeleton of a Headless Giant

Here they discovered not the coyote but the skeleton of an exceptionally tall man who'd been over seven-feet-tall and headless. Nearby was an old flintlock rifle, a decayed saddle, and, rather odd, a large number of watermelon seeds. A drinking gourd, a powder horn, and a few other items lay around the skeleton.

The discovery of the remains themselves gave no particular explanation of the mystery. It seemed clear that the former occupant of the cave apparently had died there.

But where was the skull? Had animals carried it away? If so, why had they left the rest of the bones undisturbed?

The men were debating the matter when one of them discovered a skull resting on a rocky shelf some thirty feet away from the skeleton.

Now here was a macabre mystery, indeed. The skull on the ledge could not possibly have belonged to the skeleton, for it was only about the size of a man's fist. Some alleged that it was even too small to be a baby's skull, unless the child belonged to a race of midgets.

The old-timers took all they had found to the nearest store, where they were put on exhibition for the doubtful benefit of the worthy settlers in that district, who came in scores to view the objects. There was some talk of getting an anthropologist to examine the little skull, but nothing came of the suggestion.

The Vanishing Exhibits

Then suddenly all the exhibits, except the miniature skull, vanished. Whether they vanished as the result of some paranormal phenomena or because somebody took a fancy to them has never been determined.

The next day a certain John Oxworth, living some ten miles from the store, rode there for supplies, leaving his young wife at home. When he returned, she stammered out that during his absence she had seen a strange man of enormous size riding on a black horse. His costume, she said, was that of an ancient Spanish soldier, and he rode very slowly four times around the house, stopping every few yards and slowly raising his arms up and down.

Across his saddle lay an old-fashioned flintlock rifle, and he was headless.

Mrs. Oxworth ended her story by saying that he "just faded away like fog in the sunshine."

Sightings of the Decapitated Phantom

The following day the decapitated phantom was seen by another woman some miles away. It also behaved in exactly the same manner as before, but either the phenomenon was more tangible or the woman more observant than her neighbor, for she said that the horse was foam-flecked, its mouth bloody from the cut of the Spanish-type bit.

The phantom was seen on several other occasions, one observer stating that the headless rider carried a watermelon that he slowly lifted up and down.

The leading men of the district got together and decided to explore the cave extensively in an attempt to solve the mystery, but none of them had the courage to go in first.

At this stage a brave cowpoke from the Texas Panhandle rode in and, learning of the phantom, said that he would go alone into the deepest recesses of the cave and solve the mystery once and for all.

The locals passed around a hat, and the cowpoke, lodging the dollars in his money belt, removed his spurs and entered the cave while scores of people waited outside.

That was five o'clock on a summer afternoon in the early 1890s, and from that day the brave Texan never has been seen dead or alive.

The next morning a posse of the less timid men of the North Fork area explored the outer cave but were too scared to go deeper. Not a trace of the Texan or of his six-shooter, lantern, or knife did they find.

Moreover, from that time the phantom ceased to manifest itself. Another very queer thing was that the little skull mysteriously vanished on the same day that the Texan crawled into the cave.

The haunted past still lingers over modern Oklahoma.

• 6 •

The Eternal Battles of Ghost Armies

Phantom armies and the spectral reenactments of violent battles have been witnessed by many observers throughout history.

On Christmas Day, 1692, representatives of the British king were sent to squelch "absurd rumors" that the battle of Edge Hill, which had been fought two months before, was being "refought" by phantom armies. The king's representatives returned to report that they had witnessed ghostly images so vivid, they could recognize the faces of friends who had been killed in action.

In August 1951, tourist guests and the staff of a small hotel located a mile east of Dieppe, France, observed a ghostly reenactment of the Allied landing that had taken place nine years earlier.

Areas that have served as scenes of violent activity often seem to become impregnated with a psychic residue that may continually be recharged for spectral restaging.

Phantom Defenders of the Philippines

Such a place is Corregidor, that small island in the Pacific where American and Filipino troops tried desperately to halt the Japanese advance against the city of Manila and the whole Philippine Islands. Here, according to Defense Secretary Alego S. Santos, "the defenders fought almost beyond human endurance."

Today the only living inhabitants of Corregidor's devastated island fortress are a small detachment of Filipino marines, a few firewood cutters, and a family of caretakers. These living inhabitants claim they are not alone. The island, they swear, is haunted.

Woodcutters have returned to the base screaming in terror that they have seen bleeding and wounded men running around, rifles at the ready.

Marines on jungle maneuvers say they often come face-to-face with silently stalking phantom scouts of that brutal conflict of the 1940s.

Many claim to have seen a beautiful redheaded woman moving among the ghostly wounded, ministering to their injuries. A nurse in a Red Cross uniform has also been seen appearing and disappearing in the tropical moonlight.

The night sounds are the most disconcerting to those who reside on the island. Nearly every evening is filled with horrible moans of pain and the desperate noise of marching soldiers as they race to do battle with phantom invaders.

Florentino R. Das, supervisor of tourism for Luzon, said that one night he and his wife heard the terrible sounds of men in pain. "I investigated and found nothing."

Soldiers on night duty have said that they often find themselves surrounded by rows and rows of groaning and dying men in extreme suffering. Usually this grisly scene is observed shortly after the phantom of the Red Cross nurse has been seen.

The Gurkha Ghost

When night comes to the mountains of Kashmir, the men of Fort Khamba are tense. No sentry dares sleep on duty.

The Indian army men, who guard this fort, believe that they are watched over by the Ghost of the Gurkha Havildar. And he is a harsh taskmaster.

In these mountains the legend of the Gurkha ghost has become famous. Educated army officers, although disbelieving the legend, are content to let it grow because the Gurkha ghost solves many disciplinary problems in Fort Khamba.

Indian troops swear the specter prowls the fort at night, slapping the faces of sentries who aren't alert and using his best parade-ground language to berate slovenly soldiers.

The ghost is said to be that of a Gurkha *havildar* (sergeant) who performed a heroic one-man assault on Fort Khamba during the bitter 1948 war between India and Pakistan for Kashmir. The fort, held by Pakistani forces, had fought off Indian troops for weeks. Then the Gurkha *havildar* found a crack in the fort's steep, thick stone walls and one night, armed only with grenades and a knife, crept inside. He killed all the defenders but was fatally wounded himself.

Lance Naik (*corporal*) Ram Prakash is among the fort's current defenders who say they have met the *havildar*'s ghost. It happened one night in June 1965, when firing broke out along the cease-fire line.

A terrifying voice rose, he says, from a turret on the fort's wall: "I have given my life for this post. Why are you so slack?"

Then, reported Prakash, came the sound of a face being slapped.

It was learned later, Prakash says, that a sentry in the turret was nodding over his rifle and was punished by the stern ghost.

The men of Fort Khamba say that they know the Gurkha ghost well. Each can describe in detail the clothing worn by the weird figure that strides the ramparts at night. The troops agree that the apparition invariably appears wearing only one shoe. The other apparently was lost in battle forty years ago.

"The ghost of that man is very alert," says Naik Karam Singh. "He is a very good soldier. And I guess we're really not afraid of him because we know he is on our side."

The men of Fort Khamba are very careful to put out cups of tea and sweets for the lonely Gurkha ghost, who maintains his vigil throughout the night.

And, they say, the tea and sweets are always gone by dawn.

The Phantom Marchers of Crete

"Here they come!" one of the men shouted, and pointed to a spot far down the beach. Near the edge of the water, column after column of soldiers were forming and marching toward them. As the phantom army got closer, they appeared to be tall, proud men, unlike any soldiers the men watching had ever seen. They wore metal helmets of a classic design and carried short, flat swords. They kept coming toward the men as the predawn light increased.

"Where did that woman come from?" The man who

spoke pointed at the much shorter and darker figure that seemed to be standing in the midst of the marching men.

"She works in the valley during the day," someone said, recognizing her.

The observers watched and were amazed to see the woman walk indifferently through the midst of the marching horde, seemingly unaffected by their powerful stride. The strange army marched toward the crumbling castle of the ancient Doges, and as the light of the approaching dawn increased, the last column vanished near the sea on the far side of the castle.

The men ran to the woman and asked her why she had not been afraid.

"I didn't see any marching men," she said simply.

Legion of the Shadow Men

The Phantom Marchers of Crete comprise a strange army that people from all over the island come to observe during the last weeks of May and the first week of June. Who or what makes up this eerie army has been a much-debated question by investigators of the phenomenon, as well as by the natives on the island. From the many descriptions of the spectral men that compose the army, the manner in which they are dressed, and the weapons they carry, nobody has been able to fit them into any historical setting. As for explanations of the phenomenon itself, everything from the supernatural to a mirage has been postulated.

Known as the "shadow men" or the "dew men" by the natives of the island, the as yet unexplained phenomenon always occurs just before dawn or just after sunset, and at approximately the same time of the year. They seem to come out of the sea and march directly toward the castle, then disappear with the encroaching darkness of night or the light of dawn. Any connection with the medieval Venetian castle has been written off as impossible, because the observers say that the men look like a company of soldiers marching their way right out of the pages of Homer's *Iliad*.

Reports of the phantom marches have been carried in the major Greek newspapers of Athens for almost a century. Not only Cretan peasants have reported seeing the phenomena but also a number of reputable Greek businessmen, several German archaeologists, and two English observers. An entire garrison of Turkish soldiers observed the ghostly marauders during the Turkish administration of the island in the 1870s, and were frightened into pulling out arms.

The possibility that the phantom army is a mirage has been considered and discarded by most of the theorists. A mirage has a maximum range of about forty miles and occurs only in direct sunlight. If it were a mirage, it would involve the annual staging of a secret show somewhere on the island every year at the same time for centuries, without anyone's detection. Furthermore, the phenomenon occurs in the half-light of dawn or dusk, thereby rendering the mirage theory untenable.

Marchers From an Ancient Culture

Sir Ernest Bennett, who was a classical graduate of Hertford College, Oxford University, not only believed the marchers to be a psychic manifestation of a bygone army of men but also maintained that the specters belonged to an ancient culture that once had lived on the island. Sir Ernest has collected all available reports of the phantom marchers that have circulated among the people of the island and in the newspapers of Greece. Though he spent some time on the island trying to observe the phantom marchers, they seemed to elude his detection.

The phantom column seems to be completely surrounded by a mysterious aura that makes them visible in dim light. A Cretan muleteer described them as follows.

"I was engaged by some Germans, about ten years ago, to help in some archaeological work near where they are seen. It was while I was there that many other local people and I saw these men of the shadows. It was after sunset and dark when we saw this strange army of phantoms coming across the plain toward the beach where we stood. They uttered no sound. They seemed to be in armor, and some wore strange helmets. All carried weapons, shields, short swords, and spears.

"They were all very tall men. As we looked, they seemed to vanish into the air as suddenly as they had come. It was so frightening that we were rendered dumb till the dawn came. Who can say what these shadow men are?"

Does Rommel's Ghost Haunt the Desert Battlefields?

"Ali! What in the name of the Prophet's holy eyeteeth is that out there on the far drive?"

"Where? I see nothing. Has the sun been heavy upon your eyelids today?"

"The heavy eyelids are yours, sleeper! Open them and look where I point. Perhaps what you see will awaken you!"

"Allah keep us! I see it now. It is a man—or a ghost of a man. But such a one! Look at his clothing. It is the dress of a soldier, one of those who came in the iron wagons painted with the cross."

"Shall I awaken the sheikh?"

"Yes. Go quickly—I will keep watch."

The Bedouin slipped away into the Sahara night. Ali

gathered his black robe around him and gripped his rifle. The night was cold, and white frost gave the sands an eerie air of unreality. Ali shivered, but not only from the cold. In battle or on watch, he was the bravest of men, but ghosts were something else. He spat defiantly upon the sands and took another look.

Outlined against the sky was the figure of a Nazi officer. It stood like a statue, booted feet apart hands clasped behind its back. Over the jaunty garrison cap, a pair of goggles leered like eyeless sockets. Under the left arm was tucked a baton—the mark of a German field marshal.

Ali's hands tightened on the rifle. A child of the desert, he could almost feel sound before he could hear it.

"Ali! It is I! And the sheikh!

Sheikh Ami Ben Yosef was a wise old man. Ali stood aside to allow his chief to take a better look.

"Allah be merciful!" said Ben Yosef slowly. "It is Rom-el, who is called by the English the Fox of the Desert."

"Rom-el," was better known to the men who faced his Tiger tanks during the North African campaign of World War II as Field Marshal Erwin Rommel, who later died by his own hand following an unsuccessful attempt on the life of Hitler. He still walks the sands of El Alamein, according to a report in *Psychic News*.

In May of 1942, Rommel's elite Afrika Korps, aided by Italian troops, began a powerful offensive. In a lightning-quick move Rommel captured Tobruk, Libya, and pointed the muzzles of his .88s toward Egypt. But a shortage of supplies and dogged British resistance halted Rommel's drive only sixty miles from Alexandria, at El Alamein.

In October, General Sir Bernard L. Montgomery, commanding the British Eighth Army, took the offensive and drove Rommel's forces back to Tripoli.

In the spring of 1943, United States and British forces pushed those of the Axis to the Mediterranean Sea. Rommel wired Berlin for the authority to evacuate the Afrika Korps to Nazi-occupied territory in France, in order to assist in the defense of the mainland against the Allied invasion that he knew must surely follow.

Hitler himself replied. He ordered Rommel to "fight to the death." Thus the flower of the Afrika Korps was added to the 350,000 Axis casualties of the North African campaign. But the Desert Fox escaped.

In 1944, Rommel was placed in command of a German army opposing the Allied invasion of Normandy. Shortly afterward he was called to Berlin to report personally on the progress of the war to Adolf Hitler.

Unafraid to Defy Hitler

As Rommel entered Hitler's grandiose office in the Reichstag, anger churned in his breast as he imagined the man, whom he and his fellow Prussians referred to privately as the Little Corporal, sitting at his marble-topped desk and issuing the insane order that led to the needless destruction of the Afrika Korps.

With the others he stood at attention as the führer entered.

"Sit down, gentlemen," Hitler invited magnanimously. "Rommel, how good to see you again!"

"Danke schoen, mein führer," croaked the man who might have turned the tide in an earlier hour of the great war. "It is always a pleasure to see you."

"Of course. And how are things at the front? Are we ready to drive Eisenhower and Montgomery back into the Atlantic?"

Field Marshal Rommel's eyes darted toward his friend,

von Rundstedt. Von Rundstedt looked down at the carpet. Both knew Hitler was mad.

"Nein, mein führer. The war is going against us. Patton is everywhere at once, and Montgomery falls upon us like a hungry wolf. I consider it futile to continue. I—"

"Enough! You are wrong!" Hitler screamed. "We will win! I have dreamed dreams! I have seen visions! I have seen it in the stars! Germany will win!

"Rommel, you have defied me for the last time!" the angry *führer* said, slamming an open hand on his desk. "You are relieved of your command at once! Consider yourself under arrest and do not leave Berlin. I will talk with you later."

On July 20, Colonel Count Klaus von Stauffenberg placed a time bomb under the Little Corporal's table at a staff meeting. The bomb exploded but Hitler was only injured. Erwin Rommel was implicated in the plot and was given the choice between a trial or suicide. Shortly afterward, the Desert Fox drank poison, and the war raged on.

Why does the restless spirit of "Rom-el" walk the sands of El Alamein, striking terror into the hearts of the Sahara nomads?

The battle of El Alamein was the turning point in the struggle for North Africa. Does the ghost of the Desert Fox brood over a mistake that might have changed the course of the battle and, perhaps, the war?

Or does it come to dwell fondly on the memory of the Afrika Korps' finest hour, when Rommel's tanks moved relentlessly down the road from Tobruk to Alamein?

The Civil War's Marching Ghosts

It was an unusually warm day on the afternoon of October 1, 1863, when a small group of Union soldiers stopped at the Kentucky mountaintop home of Moses Dwyer and asked for a drink of water.

"My sympathies lie elsewhere," Dwyer told the Yankees. "But I can't deny you a drink of water."

The Union sergeant thanked the mountaineer and assured him that his men would be on their best behavior if they might just rest a bit in the shade of his large porch. The members of Dwyer's family offered the troops some freshly baked cookies, and soon the civilians and the soldiers were discussing the war, as if they had forgotten the great schism that was supposed to divide them.

"Look at those strange clouds," one of the soldiers said, pointing skyward.

There, over the ridges of the adjacent hills, were rows and rows of weirdly shaped clouds, about the size and general shape of doors. They seemed to be constructed of smoke or some cottonlike substance rather than water and vapor.

"The sky is filling up with the crazy things!" said another soldier.

"And they seem to be flying on their own," noted the sergeant. "There's no wind today. How can they move like that?"

As neatly regimented as companies of soldiers, the strange clouds sailed swiftly over the heads of the astonished witnesses on the porch of the Kentucky mountain cabin. Their numbers were so great that it required more than an hour for all of the door-sized "rolls of smoke" to pass overhead.

"That be the darnedest thing I've ever seen in these mountains," Moses Dwyer said softly.

The Kentucky mountaineer had spoken too soon. Suddenly, in the valley below them, "thousands upon thousands" of what definitely seemed to be human beings appeared, marching at double time in the same direction as the "clouds."

A soldier cocked his musket nervously. "That valley is filling up with soldiers," he croaked in desperation. "The whole Rebel army is fixing to march on us, Sarge!"

The sergeant was as pale as the next man, but he had not yet allowed himself to panic. He quieted his men and spoke to them in a harsh whisper. "They ain't soldiers, but they are . . . the ghosts of men!"

The phantoms all wore white shirts and trousers and marched approximately thirty to forty "men" deep. Oblivious to the attention they were receiving from the startled mountain family and the Union troops, the apparitions strode purposefully across the valley and began to ascend the steep mountain range that surrounded it.

The ghostly marchers could have passed for a mighty earthly army on the move if it had not been for their bizarre appearance. The phantoms were not of uniform size, as their companion clouds had been. Some of the eerie marchers were tall, and others appeared to be quite small. Their legs were seen to move and their arms to swing briskly. While they marched in strict military fashion, they bore no weapons of any kind. As the phantom parade began to ascend the mountain, members of the ghostly march were seen to lean forward, just as men do when negotiating steep terrain.

It took over an hour for the great parade of phantoms to

march out of the valley, and the witnesses to the remarkable sight were left speechless and filled with wonder. Some of them, perhaps rightly, interpreted the ghostly marchers to represent the many men who would die in the bloody War Between the States.

Strangely enough, on October 14, 1863, the same parade of phantoms was observed by ten Confederate soldiers and a number of civilians at Runger's Mill, Kentucky. According to contemporary reports, the phenomenon remained identical in every detail, except that the combined passage of the weird clouds and the eerie marchers take only one hour instead of two.

• 7 •

Haunting Styles of the Rich and Famous

Very often life imitates art, and vice versa. Accomplished British actor Donald Pleasance, who in recent years has come to epitomize the very essence of the eerie, once lived in a haunted house with his family.

Pleasance, who began carving out a niche for himself in horror films with the release of the cult classic *Halloween*, has since appeared in numerous cinematic epics about hauntings and apparitions.

How did this modern master of the mysterious feel about encountering the unknown away from the cameras?

"We loved it," he said. "It was a very merry family of ghosts."

In the early 1970s Pleasance and his wife, Meira, bought a seventeenth-century home located at Strand-on-the-Green, England. Another house adjoined theirs, so they decided to buy that one, too.

"And that's when the fun started." Pleasance smiled. "We began hearing strange noises . . . thumping sounds. And although we checked throughout the house, we could not find the source of the mysterious noises.

"I was scared to death," Pleasance admitted. "But

gradually my wife and I came to realize that the sounds were distinctly those of children running.

"Then it hit us—when we knocked down the walls, we'd allowed the ghosts of children once again to run through the house, as they'd probably done many years before when they were alive and it was all one big house."

Once the Pleasance family had determined the origin of the thumps and bumps, they had no problem with the concept of sharing their home with the ghosts.

"The sounds were, after all, sounds of joy. We could feel the happiness of the children. They seemed happy to have a free run of the place after all those centuries."

The Actor Who Gets His Lines From the Other Side

Patrick Waddington is one of the most versatile and well-known character actors of British stage, screen, and television.

The former singer turned actor has freely discussed some of the psychic experiences that have shared equal billing with acting in his life.

Waddington is a natural clairaudient, although until 1968, he had never studied Spiritualism. All he knew was that he heard voices, and the voices always spoke the truth. He associates the voices with ill health, as they always come through clearest and most frequently when he is running a fever.

On an American tour some years ago with Ray Milland's production of *Hostile Witness,* he heard his psychic warning voice. Distinctly it told him to remove his valuables from the top tray of his trunk.

Obediently the actor got up and began to carry out the

voice's order. Then, weakened with fever, he decided he had imagined the voice and abandoned his task.

The next night, during the last performance in Milwaukee, Wisconsin, there was a robbery. The troupe's luggage had been stacked in the hotel's back alley, ready for departure, and of the whole lot, only Patrick Waddington's trunk—probably because it was the smallest and most portable—was stolen.

On a previous occasion Waddington heeded the voice, and, though under unfortunate conditions, he was glad he did. On vacation, the actor was sitting atop a cliff enjoying his solitude. In the water below, his eyes languidly followed the path of a canoe being paddled by two boys. All at once a voice spoke sharply in his ear. You must do something, they are going to drown!"

Patrick whirled around, in search of the person who had spoken. Seeing no one, he realized it had to have been his "voice."

Spurred into action, the actor ran half a mile to the nearest coast guard station. When he got there, he learned that rescue operations had already been initiated to retrieve the boy's bodies. The canoe had overturned and both of them had drowned.

One cannot simply assume that Patrick Waddington's voices are the result of a delirious, feverish imagination, because the message it brought regarding his trunk, had it been heeded, certainly would have prevented Waddington from losing his valuables. And though he did not make it to the coast guard station in time to save the lives of the two young canoers, at least the information was correct. It truly appears that Patrick Waddington receives commands from other than earthly stage directors.

Elke Sommer's Haunted House

Glamorous German-born actress Elke Sommer capped off a series of personal mystical experiences when she and her husband, writer Joe Hyams, moved into a haunted house in July 1964. The strange happenings in this house have been recounted both in magazines and in a book by Hyams.

Elke and Joe were told by the previous tenants that the house was inhabited by a spirit wearing a black jacket. At first neither of them believed that they had moved in with a ghost. Soon footsteps, scuffling and scraping noises, and dining room chairs that moved, began to change their minds. Before long the ghostly tenant even made brief appearances in his black jacket.

The phenomena continued in the house, plaguing not only Elke and Joe but the people to whom they later sublet the home. Then, on March 20, 1966, Joe Hyams phoned a well-known psychic sensitive, Jacqueline Eastlund, and asked her to solve the mystery of his haunted house.

Joe placed the receiver of the telephone on the table so that Mrs. Eastlund could pick up the psychic vibrations in the house.

When the two spoke again, Mrs. Eastlund informed Hyams that he should be careful because she saw "the house in flames within six months. I also hear the sound of a rainfall and a kind of tapping."

A year later, on March 13, 1967, Elke woke during a heavy rainfall at about six A.M. She was troubled with a vague uneasiness. As she listened to the rain she became aware of sounds downstairs. The longer she listened, the stronger she felt an inexplicable dread and an intense impulse to move around.

Anxiously she awakened her husband, and just as she was trying to describe the sounds downstairs they were both startled by yet another sound—a loud and insistent pounding on the bedroom door.

Leaping to the door, Joe pulled it open and was almost overcome by the hot, black cloud of smoke that billowed into the room. The house was a burning inferno, and their access to the hall was cut off.

Hyams slammed the door shut and quickly called the fire department. Then he and Elke desperately looked around for a means of escape.

While doing this they were again directed by the pounding. This time it came from the window, and when Elke ran to look out, she immediately realized that by climbing through it she and Joe could jump to the roof of the garage and from there easily drop to the ground.

Had not Joe and Elke been awakened and guided by the ghostly pounding, they would have been consumed by the flames.

Valentino's Death Ring

In 1964 I began working on a biography of the great silent screen star Rudolph Valentino. This book, published in 1966, was based in part on the remembrances of a fascinating gentleman named Chaw Mank, who had headed the great lover's fan club. In 1977, the book served as the basis for the Ken Russell, Valentino, film that starred ballet-master Rudolph Nureyev as Valentino and featured Michelle Phillips, Leslie Caron, and Carol Kane.

Chaw was a confidant to many stars in the motion picture, recording, and television industries. In his psychic diary of the stars he disclosed many ghostly experiences that had occurred to a number of legendary performers. Chaw died in 1987.

Valentino, who was famous for dancing the tango, and Chaw Mank were both at the height of popularity when Chaw Mank traveled to Chicago to chat with the great lover of the silent screen, who was touring and waiting out a disagreement with his studio. Mank told his idol how he and his dance partner had won a number of contests doing the tango.

"Why," Chaw said with a gasp, "someone was even silly enough to dazzle a contract in front of our eyes!"

"You might become the next romantic star on silver screen," Valentino teased him.

"Naw," Chaw told the movie star. "I'm too interested in my music. Besides, a fellow never knows what tomorrow will bring.

"It was then that I saw the strange cat's-eye ring on Valentino's finger," Chaw recalled.

" 'Hey, Rudy,' I said, 'you've picked up a new bauble since last I saw you.' "

Valentino smiled as he slipped the ring off his finger and offered it to Chaw for appraisal.

"I picked it up in San Francisco's Chinatown," he told him. "The old shopkeeper who sold it to me called it a destiny ring. What," Valentino asked, narrowing his large eyes and lowering his voice to a whisper, "do you see as my destiny?"

Chaw tried to resist the shudder that suddenly had beset him. It seemed that the handsome features of the screen lover had become contorted and pale. The smoldering sensuality of the movie star seemed displaced by a deathly pallor.

Mank gasped when he saw a vision of his idol in a scene of violent and painful death.

"What is it?" Valentino asked, frowning his concern for his young friend's strange behavior. "Another of your predictions? Well, I shall ignore you this time. The old Chinaman told me that it would bring me good luck."

"Yes," Chaw agreed. "The ring will bring you good luck. I see your career taking an upswing very soon. I see you settling your difference with Famous Players Studio and working out a better deal with another studio, but . . ." Chaw hesitated as the vision of violent death once more clouded his thoughts.

"Then the ring *is* lucky." Valentino smiled. "If all these things are going to happen, why do you look so glum? Cheer up!"

Valentino's career did climb to new heights, and he was often heard to refer to the cat's-eye as his good-luck ring.

Chaw's vision did come true, however. Valentino was wearing the destiny ring when he died painfully from a gastric ulcer perforating on a hot August day in 1926. Valentino had driven himself too hard, ignoring the admonitions of his own body. Although the official cause of the screen star's death was attributed to blood poisoning, the great celluloid lover's demise is shrouded in mystery and rumors that the "perforations" in his intestines were caused by ground glass or a bullet wound.

The popular singer Russ Columbo was signed by a Hollywood studio to portray Rudolph Valentino on the screen. The next time Chaw saw the cat's-eye, it was on Columbo's ring finger. He had fallen heir to the ring, along with an assignment to impersonate the great movie lover.

"That ring was meant only for Valentino," Chaw Mank

told the singer. "You know, Russ, I wouldn't wear that ring if I were you. Valentino said it would bring him good luck. I agreed, but I tried to warn him that it would also bring him violent death."

Columbo teased him for indulging in mumbo-jumbo superstition, but Mank reflects, "I wonder if Russ had time for second thoughts. He was killed in an automobile accident just before he was to start filming the life of Valentino."

Joe Casino, a close friend of Columbo's, was next to inherit the strange cat's-eye ring. Casino put the ring on display but told everyone that he would not wear the bauble until he was certain the curse had had time to wear off.

The destiny ring lay in a display case for several years before Casino reckoned it was safe to slip the cat's-eye on his finger. A few days later Casino was struck and killed by a truck.

Today the Valentino "death ring" is thought to be in the possession of a New York barber, who won the ring in a radio contest to determine which listener could write the best letter on the mysterious, tragic properties of the cat's-eye. One can only hope that if the strange bauble was ever truly a "death ring," its deadly properties have at last been dissipated.

Did Valentino's Ghost Haunt Falcon Lair?

Shortly after the great screen lover's untimely death, eerie stories began to circulate about Rudolph Valentino's ghost haunting his favorite places. Falcon Lair, the dream home he had built for his bride, became the most commonly reported site for ectoplasmic manifestations of the departed Valentino.

Those screen fans whose worship of the Great Lover approached idolatry themselves began to haunt the grounds in hope of catching a glimpse of Valentino's ghost. The more important and persistent of the faithful somehow managed to wrangle invitations to stay the night in the glamorous mansion. A chosen few were fortunate enough to spend the night in Valentino's own bedroom.

Like children awaiting a visit from Santa Claus, the excited and expectant fans would lie there, ready to receive and transcribe any messages Rudy might choose to deliver from beyond the grave. All of Valentino's "faithful" knew that he firmly believed in the possibility of the return of the spirit, and if his shade did not manifest itself on the particular evening in which they were privileged to spend a night in Falcon Lair, they concluded that the fault lay either with themselves or with adverse spiritual conditions in the atmosphere.

One story about the appearance of Valentino's ghost involved a caretaker, who ran down the canyon in the middle of the night, screaming at the top of his lungs that he had seen Rudy.

Another popular legend told of a stable man who left the grounds without collecting his belongings when he had seen the ghost of the master petting his favorite horse at sunset one evening.

The myth makers made a great deal of the fact that the New York jeweler who had won the bid for Falcon Lair later backed out of the transaction. Those who supposedly knew the details claimed that the restless spirit of Rudolph Valentino had not wished to be usurped by the physical presence of one who dealt in such materialistic items as jewelry.

A woman from Seattle was visiting the caretakers of Falcon Lair, and claimed that she had been alone in the mansion writing a letter when she heard muffled footsteps and saw doors open and close. She had been completely alone in the house except for Rudy and Brownie, Valentino's two favorite watchdogs—trained to back or snap at everyone . . . except their master. Strangely, the dogs didn't bark, they only whimpered at what may have been their master's footsteps.

The Spirit That Warned
Jean Harlow of Death

"I see someone with light blond hair around you—a young girl who is very famous," said the Spiritualist Chaw Mank was visiting in St. Louis. "You and she write to each other, but all of a sudden this writing will stop. She will never again dip her pin in ink."

Chaw listened with sadness to the prediction as the lovely face of his pen pal, Jean Harlow, visited his mind's eye. He, too, had felt a terrible sense of foreboding surrounding Jean's life, and he regretted having another psychic confirmation.

Jean and Chaw had been corresponding for some time, and Chaw felt honored that the platinum-blond glamour queen poured out to him so many of her innermost thoughts. It taught him that she had a beautiful mind to complement her looks, and her constant acts of kindness revealed the generosity of her heart.

Jean loved white and each year sent out white Christmas cards to her friends and fans. Chaw was always on her list. From these and from the many personal letters she sent him, Chaw was able to pick up Jean's vibrations and get to know her better.

"Jean's life was not the bed of roses the press releases

made it out to be," Chaw declared. "She had too many obstacles to fight and conquer. I could tell from her many letters that Jean loved life, but at times she gave the impression of being a butterfly caught in a spiderweb. She was restless and always wondered what would become of her. She was obsessed with the future, along with the heartbreak and hardship she knew it would bring. Jean had a very realistic outlook on life.

"I have always thought that the only man she really loved was Clark Gable. To me their love scenes were more deeply rooted in fact than any I have seen, with the only possible exception of John Gilbert and Greta Garbo. Yet to Jean, Gable was more of a protecting angel, an institution of wisdom and kindness.

"It is difficult to talk about the loves of Jean Harlow. They would just happen. Above all else she was Jean—she was herself—and seemed to have an inner knowledge that she would not be long-lived. This is why she had to give what love she had while she could."

This inkling of her untimely death pervaded the letters she sent to Chaw, who could sense it clearly. As the appointed time approached, the tone of her letters changed. To Chaw it seemed as though she were no longer living here but simply visiting.

In her final letters to Chaw, Jean admitted that she had been talking to someone in the spirit world—someone she did not know—and that the entity had told her to prepare for death. Finally, six months after she told Chaw of her visions, Jean Harlow bade farewell to the world and died.

Abe Lincoln's White House Spooks

While a great deal of media attention was stirred up by suggestions that President Ronald Reagan and First Lady Nancy were devotees of astrology, imagine the feeding frenzy among journalists if it had been discovered that there were mediums and channelers in the White House. Such was the case of Abraham Lincoln, who openly conducted regular séances.

The winter of 1863 was harsh. A new Union general had taken command of the haggard Yankee forces. The morale of the troops was at its lowest ebb since the war had begun. Sensing the critical situation, Washington D.C. had taken on a serious, almost solemn, air.

In Cranston Laurie's Georgetown drawing room, the firelight flickered faintly across the floor and off the faces of the several people gathered there. All attention in the room was riveted on the frail body of medium Nettie Colburn, resting easily in a leather chair. Her breathing was shallow and, from a distance, almost imperceptible. A man swung a gold watch in front of her eyes and counted softly with the pendulumlike swings.

Finally he stuffed the watch back into his vest pocket and let the chain drape across his brightly colored vest. "All we can do now is wait." His voice was subdued.

The atmosphere in the room grew tense as each moment passed. The silence became a burden to the people there. Then, after five minutes, the head of the semiconscious girl moved slightly. In another instant her whole body began to quiver. She was in a trance.

"Remedy the situation by going in person to the front

with your wife and family." The voice, a startling deep bass, rolled out of the girl's mouth. Those in the room were initially astounded by the voice, then began to pay attention to the content of Nettie Colburn's speech.

The people in the room formed a tight, intense circle around the high-backed leather chair—Cranston Laurie, Mrs. Miller, Daniel E. Somes, Mrs. Laurie, and President Abraham Lincoln.

The president, who sought to heal his divided country, listened intently to a plan for increasing troop morale as it came from another dimension through the mouth of a frail young woman. The next day, plans for Lincoln's visit to the wintering Union troops were announced.

Abraham Lincoln, one of the most revered presidents of the United States, was constantly chided by the newspapers of his time for his consultations with the spirit world. The Cleveland *Plain Dealer* lashed at him shortly after his election to the presidency for "consulting spooks."

The then president-elect's candid reply was: "The only falsehood in the statement is that the half of it has not been told. The article does not begin to tell the wonderful things I have witnessed."

Seeking Spiritual Help to Shape Executive Policies

Openly and admittedly, Abe Lincoln consulted mediums and Spiritualists of his day. Historians and biographers make little fuss about recording that he had inherited a strong spiritual heritage from his mother and her family. The consultations varied from those received from backwoods Gypsies, when he was in his youth, to the most famous mediums and telepaths of the day during his tenure as president. Reared in an atmosphere where people listened closely to advice from the spiritual world, he was never a skeptic but used these contacts in shaping his policies as chief executive.

Nettie Colburn, and other mediums with whom Lincoln kept in close communication, would allow their bodies to become vehicles for whatever force took them over, spewing forth information that the thoughtful president considered with all the energy of his serious nature. Other participants in these spirit-summoning sessions were Senator Richmond, Colonel S. P. Kase, Major Vanvorhees, and First Lady Mary Todd Lincoln. Daniel E. Somes, a frequent séance partner, was a congressman at the time.

In times of great crisis the president's wife would arrange séances to calm her husband. Some of the gatherings took place in the White House itself.

In December 1862, the Union cause was on the brink of defeat. Lincoln was under great strain, and Mrs. Lincoln called several people together in the Red Room. Once again Nettie Colburn was the medium. In her own words she described what had taken place:

"For more than an hour, I was made to talk to Mr. Lincoln. I learned from my friends afterward that it was upon matters that he seemed fully to understand, while the others comprehended very little until the portion was reached that related to the forthcoming Emancipation Proclamation."

Daniel Webster's Counsel From the Other Side

Lincoln had been under great pressure from all sides to drop his rigid support of the Emancipation Proclamation. In trance, Nettie Colburn told him he was charged not to compromise the terms at all but to resolutely carry out all the implications of the announcement he had made.

According to Nettie Colburn, after she had come out of the trance she found the president looking intently at her, his arms folded across his chest. A gentleman present asked Lincoln if he had noticed anything familiar about the voice and delivery of the message.

"Mr. Lincoln raised himself as if shaking off a spell. He glanced quickly at the full-length portrait of Daniel Webster that hung over the piano and replied, 'Yes, and it is very singular, very!'"

It seems that Lincoln heeded the spirit world's admonition, for the Emancipation Proclamation became effective a few weeks later on January 1, 1863.

Lincoln admitted that the messages he received from the spirit world enabled him to come through crisis after crisis. His influence extended to other figures of the time, and even the hard-nosed Ulysses S. Grant later turned to Spiritualism. Never before or since has the spirit world had so much influence in Washington.

• 8 •

Ghosts on College Campuses

Based on numerous reports, it would seem that the ghost of a girls' college headmistress still haunts the school she founded more than a hundred years ago.

Lars Hoffman, of Lewis and Clark Community College in Godfrey, Illinois, has stated that there have been hundreds of incidents involving the ghost of Harriet Haskell, who ran Monticello College, a school for girls, at the site of the present college. The presence of the spirit is most often felt in the library—where Ms. Haskell held daily chapel services and lay in state after her death.

When I accepted an invitation to investigate the phenomenon, I was told that librarians had felt hands on their shoulders; sensed eyes following them around the room; and heard voices, shrieks, and moans. Custodians had reported elevators running up and down, the lights and water fountains going on and off, and furniture being moved.

Students told me of having been confronted in darkened hallways by the form of a woman in a long black skirt and a white, high-collared blouse. One student said that she had glanced up from her studies in the library to see the image of an older woman at prayer. When the woman faded from her view, she was startled and convinced that she had had a paranormal experience.

Professor Hoffman told journalist Paul Bannister that female students had told of seeing apparitions at the foots of their beds. Others said that they had seen eerie images in their mirrors.

Hoffman once called in psychic-sensitive Greta Alexander, who had a fine record of cooperating in police investigations. "I took Greta into a suite of rooms and asked if she felt anything," Hoffman said. "She immediately felt for her face and said that she felt searing pain on the left side. That was the side of Harriet's face that had been badly burned and scarred on Christmas Eve when she had played Santa for a group of girls in her suite and her whiskers had caught on fire."

Later Greta stated that she saw a woman in a long black skirt. "Harriet's ghost is there, watching over the college she loved," she concluded.

St. Louis psychic-sensitive Beverly Jaegers has been called to the college on several occasions. "I'm convinced the hauntings are real," she said. "The first time I went there, I met a woman in a long black skirt wearing a white high-collared blouse with a pin at the neck. She had scars on one side of her face. I knew she was not of this world, and as I approached, she faded away silently."

Although I did not personally witness any dramatic phenomenon during my stay at the college, I spoke to a good number of students who sincerely related their interaction with an entity they deemed to be Harriet Haskell. I could only conclude that the incidents at Lewis and Clark Community College constitute a bona fide haunting, and that somehow the ghost of Harriet Haskell still walks the halls of the girls' school she loved so much.

Strange Occurrences at St. Paul School of Art

Before Carl Weschcke purchased the ninety-year-old mansion on Summit Avenue in St. Paul, Minnesota, it had been occupied by the St. Paul School and Gallery of Art. Although the mansion had a long history of strange occurrences, the first evidence Weschcke had of its mysterious past was when he found an upper-floor window that simply would not stay closed. Even when he nailed the window shut, he would find it open the next time he visited the room.

When Weschcke was remodeling the house, a workman reported seeing a shadowy figure on an upper floor.

When he moved into the mansion Weschcke heard strange noises in the night. He could identify the unmistakable sounds of footsteps moving in hallways, people coughing, doors being shut—yet he was certain he was completely alone at all times when these audible manifestations occurred.

The ghosts did not walk only at night. One afternoon, when Weschcke was alone in the library, he turned to see the figure of a man standing in the doorway, no more than ten feet from him.

In relating the incident Weschcke has said: "Neither of us moved. There was no sound. We just kept standing face-to-face. He wore a dark suit. His face was long and thin. His hair was bushy and white. He seemed to have an expression of surprise when he saw me. I think we must have stood there for about thirty seconds. The figure simply faded away. It didn't turn a corner. It just evaporated, and then there was nothing."

Malcolm Lien, who once headed the school that was housed in Weschcke's home and who later became director of the St. Paul Art Center, remembered that many of his teachers had sensed the presence of "ghosts" in the building.

"These people were sound, educated, and well read. Yet many had this feeling of some kind of supernatural or unknown thing in the building," Lien said.

Dr. Delmar Kolb, director of the Museum of New Mexico in Santa Fe, remembered the time when he'd lived in an apartment in the mansion. Dr. Kolb was certain that he will always carry the memory of the evening when he felt two fingers on his forehead.

"I was in a cold sweat," he said. "I reached for the light, but when I turned it on, there was a blue flash and the room was dark."

Dr. Kolb stated that he did not sleep the rest of the night.

Two days later, when he opened a cupboard door to get a paper bag, the bag leapt out and hopped across the kitchen floor. There was no mouse inside, and there was no draft in the room.

"A short time later," the artist said, "I awoke to see a figure at the foot of my bed."

At first Kolb thought he had surprised an intruder rummaging in his apartment. The thin figure was dressed in black, but Kolb was surprised by the top hat the man wore.

"He moved away from me and faded, evaporating through a solid brick wall."

It was not long afterward that he moved out of the mansion.

Two college students occupied the room after Dr. Kolb had retreated from the unknown. Although the students did not know of their predecessor's experiences, one of them reported seeing the floating face of a child above his head.

A student in another room in the mansion told a staff member that he had seen the head of a man floating in his apartment.

Carl Weschcke, who is now comfortably adjusted to the four-story mansion and has made it his home, said that he is no longer bothered by the ghosts. "I just take whatever is there for granted," he commented. "I feel that they have come to accept me."

Father Lesches Still Walks at St. Mary's

At St. Mary's college in Winona, Minnesota, students in Heffron Hall annually report strange tapping noises up and down the hall at odd hours of the night.

"It's just the ghost of Father Lesches tapping about with his cane," the knowledgeable student will tell the less well informed.

Numerous students and faculty have also reported the existence of "cold spots" in the hall and in other areas of the building. In the jargon of the ghost hunter, "cold spots" are said to manifest themselves in dwellings said to be afflicted with ghostly visitors of one kind or another. Such icy areas are regarded as the core of any phenomena existing in that building.

These reports brought in psychical researchers equipped with sensitive measuring devices of varied descriptions and talents. During a stay of ten days the investigators found that at one forty-five A.M. each evening the temperature dropped as much as ten degrees in the areas of the "cold spots." It was learned that Father Lesches died between one-thirty and two A.M.

The legend of the Ghost of Heffron Hall began in 1915,

when Father Lawrence M. Lesches attempted to murder Bishop Patrick R. Heffron. Father Lesches had been turned down repeatedly in his requests for a parish of his own, and it was thought that he must have suffered a mental breakdown and focused the blame for his rejections upon Bishop Heffron.

At his trial Father Lesches was judged legally insane and committed to the Hospital for the Dangerously Insane at St. Peter, Minnesota. Although he was later pronounced sane, the clergyman was never released and died in the asylum in 1943.

But even before Father Lesches's death, the campus of St. Mary's was the scene of eerie and bizarre happenings.

In 1931, Father Edward W. Lynch, a close friend of Bishop Heffron and a known opponent of Father Lesches, was found dead, sprawled across his bed in such a manner that his body and the bed formed a cross.

Although Father Lynch's death presented mystery enough in itself, it was the condition of the cleric's body that really brought in the world of the weird. The corpse was charred to a crisp, but there was not a trace of fire anywhere else in the room. Not even the bed itself bore the slightest trace of flames.

The priest's prayer book was the only other object in the room that had also fallen victim to the mysterious fire. According to witnesses, only one passage in the entire book could be made out: "And the Lord shall come again to the sounding of trumpets."

Those who knew both Father Lynch and Father Lesches shuddered when they heard which particular passage had survived the consuming flames. During one of their numerous arguments Father Lesches had repeated a Biblical passage to Father Lynch: "And the Lord shall come again to the sounding of trumpets."

GHOSTS AMONG US

No one was ever able to explain Father Lynch's death. In that same decade another priest died in a campus fire, and three others went to flaming death in an airplane crash.

In a poll taken of St. Mary's students in 1968, it was learned that more than half of those questioned believed that some strange thing walks in the night in Heffron Hall.

An Image of the Past at Nebraska Wesleyan

On October 23, 1963, Mrs. Coleen Buterbaugh was walking across the campus of Nebraska Wesleyan, where she was secretary to Dr. Sam Dahl, dean of the college.

At exactly eight-fifty A.M., she entered the old C. C. White Building, which is used primarily as a music hall. Her heels clicked softly as she walked down a long corridor to her office at the end. Yawning, whispering students were changing their first class for either another class or a cup of morning coffee. Mrs. Buterbaugh entered the office of Dr. Tom McCourt, a visiting lecturer from Scotland. It was, she mused to herself, a typical early-morning scene at Nebraska Wesleyan. But what waited for Coleen Buterbaugh in Dr. McCourt's office was far from typical.

As she stepped into the two-room suite, Mrs. Buterbaugh was struck by an almost overwhelming odor of musty air. When she opened the door to the office, she had observed that both rooms were empty and that the windows were open.

"I had the strange feeling that I was not in the office alone," she later told Rose Sipe of the Lincoln *Evening Journal*. "I looked up and, for what must have been just a few seconds, saw the figure of a woman standing at a cabinet with her back to me in the second office. She was reaching up into one of the drawers."

Mrs. Buterbaugh could no longer hear the noisy babble of students in the outer hall as they passed from their classes. She had the eerie feeling that she had suddenly become isolated from reality.

The "other" secretary, who seemed to be filing cards so industriously, was tall, slender, and dark-haired. Her clothing was definitely of another period—a long-sleeved white shirtwaist and an ankle-length brown skirt.

"I still felt that I was not alone," Mrs. Buterbaugh told the newswoman. "I felt the presence of a man sitting at the desk to my left, but as I turned around there was no one there.

"I gazed out the large window behind the desk, and the scenery seemed to be what it might have been many years ago. There were no streets. The new Willard sorority house that now stands across the lawn was not there. Nothing outside was modern.

"By then I was frightened, so I turned and left the room!"

Mrs. Buterbaugh hurried back to her desk in Dean Dahl's office. She sat down at her typewriter, fitted the Dictaphone plug to her ear, and tried to work on the letters the dean had dictated. It was no good. Her nervous, shaking fingers refused to obey the recorded voice of her boss. She decided that she simply must tell the story to someone. It was too much for her to keep to herself.

When she entered the dean's office, he rose to his feet and helped her to a chair, for she seemed so pale and shaken.

He listened to her story, and then, without comment, asked her to accompany him to the office of Dr. Glenn Callan, chairman of the Division of Social Sciences, who has been on the Wesleyan faculty since 1900. Again Mrs.

Buterbaugh was fortunate enough to find a listener who heard her out and treated her story with respect.

After carefully quizzing Mrs. Buterbaugh and piecing together a number of clues from her strange tale of a step into the past, Dr. Callan concluded that the secretary had somehow managed to "walk" into the office as it had been at some time in the 1920s. The apparition she had seen had undoubtedly been that of Miss Clara Mills, whose office it then was. Miss Mills had come to Wesleyan as head of the Music Department and was an instructor in piano and music appreciation. She had been found dead in her office in the late 1930s.

The Schoolmaster's Lady Ghost

J. Edward Thomas is director of the largest English-language school in Spain, and he has always ridiculed the existence of ghosts and hauntings, which he sees as nonsense. Yet the director of the British Institute is embarrassed to admit that he once had a lady ghost on his hands.

Thomas is a matter-of-fact Australian who edited scientific journals in London before he traveled through Spain in 1957 and decided to invest in a language school in Cordoba. Later he bought out the school's owner, opened another school in Cadi, then joined the British Institute in Seville in 1962. Today Thomas directs a teaching program that tutors over a thousand Spaniards and several hundred students from other areas of the globe.

For the last ten years Thomas has been residing in a two-story sixteenth-century palace, which is also the Institute's home and houses the school's nine-thousand-volume library of English books. It was during the winter of 1964 that Thomas saw the palace ghost for the first time.

"I happened to be looking through the glass in the door," he told correspondent Nino Lo Bello, "and I saw her walking down the stairs. When she stepped onto the patio, she disappeared. She made not a sound, nor did she speak. But she was plain as could be. From the way she was dressed, I would judge her as a woman from the 1920s."

Thomas remembered that the ghost appeared around eight P.M. on a January night. "Unfortunately," he added, "no one else saw her."

But two years later, in January 1966, almost to the very day, the lady ghost returned at approximately the same time in the evening, and Thomas saw her again.

"She was all in gray," he recalled for the journalist, "but very, very pretty. Once again she vanished."

The pretty phantom did not show up in January 1968, and the next time Thomas saw her was in January 1969.

"I was all alone again, in the same place, and still as sober as I have ever been," Thomas stated. "I was determined to speak with her, but as soon as I opened my mouth, she disappeared instantly. I cannot tell you how frightfully disappointed I was. I wanted so much to get to know her."

Thomas confessed that he kept an eye out for his ghost every day from the same spot on the patio near the head of the stairs. He has seen her three times.

"I still don't believe in such things," he said, "but nevertheless, I have no intentions of giving up my ghost!"

Thomas admitted that the ghost of the lovely lady had begun not only to disturb him but to fascinate him.

"I am trying very hard to bring about a meeting to make

her acquaintance," he said soberly. "I have had the Seville police in several times to inspect the place minutely, but they have found no trace whatsoever of anything that could solve the mystery."

▪ 9 ▪

Chicago—America's Most Haunted City

I recall an incident that occurred in the Division Street apartment of Rosemarie "Bud" Stewart, when one of the unseen denizens that help make Chicago America's most haunted city put in a rather dramatic appearance. Present for the unscheduled performance psychic-sensitive Joseph DeLouise and his wife; Mrs. Stewart and her son, Jeb; my secretary, Jeanyne; Robert Cummings, a Canadian broadcast journalist; and myself.

I was seated a bit apart from the group in a large easy chair. Due to the arrangement of the room, I was the only one who was able to see down the long hallway that led to Bud Stewart's dining room and kitchen.

As I sat deeply engrossed in conversation with Joseph, I became gradually aware of footsteps approaching me down the hallway. Although I did notice the sounds, I did not turn around, because I assumed I would see either Jeanyne or Jeb approaching me. I was vaguely aware that neither of them was present in the living room, but I had been so involved in talking that I had not taken notice when Bud had sent Jeanyne and Jeb on an errand.

The footsteps were quite loud, very natural-sounding. When at last I did turn to acknowledge the presence of whoever was so firmly approaching me, I was quite amazed to see no one at all.

I blurted some small sound of wonderment, and the footsteps turned to make a hasty, noisy retreat.

My sudden exclamation directed the attention to everyone in the room to the sound of the running footsteps of an unseen entity. Bud Stewart ran back to her kitchen in time to observe the door of the refrigerator swing open unassisted.

Although our action seemed a bit superfluous, we went through the motions of checking all the doors and windows to see that no intruder could have physically entered the room.

In retrospect this bit of rational precaution seems a bit silly. I had a clear view down the long hallway, so I surely should have seen any physical person approaching me or running away from me, had such a person indeed existed.

A few moments after we had returned to the front room the sound of footsteps was once again heard coming down the hallway. As before, I was seated where I could command a long view of the hall. The tread of the invisible thing continued until it reached a large cabinet in the hallway, then it stopped and ran back to the kitchen once more, as if we terrible human creatures might be chasing it.

During this repeat performance, however, we were all able to hear what appeared to be the mumbling of several voices in the kitchen. None of us claimed to be able to distinguish any words, only a jumble of soft voices. Bud found that the refrigerator door had popped open, as before.

There were no further manifestations that evening, but as we discussed the incident Bud admitted that she had heard unusual sounds in the apartment before that evening's impressive display. On a number of occasions, she said, she had glimpsed the image of "someone" in the hallway. It seemed to me as though the mediumship of Joseph DeLouise, coupled with the apparent sensitivity of Bud Stewart, had activated the residue of whatever ghostly manifestation was pocketed in that apartment.

The "Vibes" Are Right in Chicago

Why does Joseph DeLouise believe paranormal phenomena are so common in Chicago?

"The vibes are here," he answered firmly. "We're either being bombarded with the right gamma rays or the right vibrations or *something* here. The vibes here are just right for growth in the psychic and religious fields. Right now Chicago is a city of psychic receivers, and their channels have been opened because of these spiritual vibrations.

"As I travel around the country I tune in and I get different vibrations. In some areas I don't seem to be as effective as others. But when I come back to Chicago, everything starts to work better.

"Certain areas seem to drain a person's psychic energies. Chicago replenishes them. And I'm seeing more and more people becoming affected in this way. The Chicago area has the vibrations conducive to psychic development, psychic research, and psychic phenomena—the entire spectrum of psi activity.

"And I'm talking about the man in the street as much as I am the professional psychic. I say that if a person is interested in developing his psychic abilities, his channels would open faster in Chicago than in certain other places. I mean, it's like transplanting a flower from one area to another; in some areas it will grow more, in some areas it will grow less. People are going to grow better and faster psychically in Chicago.

"It has something to do with clouds, the altitude of the city, and the water in the lake that make the chemistry and the vibrations just right. I'm not a scientist. I'm only speaking intuitively."

Haunted Mansions and Spooky Apartments

When I accompanied psychic-sensitive Irene Hughes on a one-day psychic safari to a large, sprawling mansion just outside Chicago, and as I listened to the sounds of a ghost child singing in an abandoned upstairs room, I was again impressed by the naturalness of haunting phenomena.

There were other times with Irene when the phenomena took such bizarre turns that impressions of eeriness, perhaps tinged with downright uneasiness (should I admit dread?), caused me to take greater note of factors other than the naturalness of the manifestation. In other instances, with medium Deon Frey, with psychic Olof Jonsson, the phenomena became extremely active, and psychokinetic effects set furniture and other objects in motion.

Richard T. Crowe, an expert on spontaneous phenomena, has said that the odds of seeing a ghost in the city of Chicago are probably greater than anywhere else in the world.

"Apparitions and spirits roam the streets and cemeteries and haunt houses," Crowe commented. "We even have a ghost house here in Chicago—a house that appears and disappears in the dark of night. This ghostly dwelling is near Bachelor's Grove Cemetery, an abandoned burial ground off 143rd Street, near Midlothian.

"As if the thing were not mystery enough," Crowe went on, "old records show that there *never* has been a house there. But the ghost house appears on either side of the road, in different places. Witnesses always describe it in the same way: wooden columns, a porch swing, and a dim light glowing within."

Crowe said that no one had ever claimed to have entered the ghostly domicile, but he added grimly: "Perhaps those who do never return to tell about it."

During the early 1970s I did many a late-night talk show with my good friend Ed "Chicago" Schwartz on WIND radio, and the listeners who telephone to contribute their own stories during the call-in portion of the program provided me with dozens of remarkable first-person accounts of their own encounters with haunted Chicago.

Of course, an old pro like Ed had heard more than his share of fantastic accounts from members of the "kook-and-crackpot" crowd, who clutch their radios to their bosoms as their late-night friend. Many of these men and women, in a desperate move to banish loneliness, somehow summon the courage to dial the telephone and lay an incredible tale on Ed—two parts remembered *Twilight Zone* episode, three parts old story Grandpa used to tell, one part fleeting memory of an old movie matinee serial, and one part the contribution of their own imaginations. But seriously, they are actually saying it over the radio and zillions of people are hearing *their* story!

Ed could recognize such frustration-born, self-deluded, thrilling wonder stories as quickly as I could, but there were many sincere men and women who truly provided us with what sound like authentic experiences—with everything from mysterious lights in cemeteries to phantom hitchhikers; from haunted lovers' lanes to ghostly footsteps in the attic; from mysterious moans in the closet to apparitions of a loved one at the moment of his or her death.

Séances With Olof Jonsson

I was not aware of any "invisible beings" at the séance that I attended in the home of Ted M., a Chicago-area schoolteacher, in which Ruth Zimmerman and Olof Jonsson served as mediums, but the table did become quite lively and, unfortunately, dealt the soft-spoken and gentle Mrs. Zimmerman a severe blow in the abdomen as it rocked violently on its side. The low blow seemed to end the table dance for that night, but Mrs. Zimmerman did attract a number of glowing, firefly-size lights around her face, and there were a few raps on the table's surface.

Ruth Zimmerman is one of Olof Jonsson's favorite "batteries." That is to say, the two mediums are "harmonious," to use Olof's pet term; they work well together. Ruth is a medium of no small ability herself, but she is one of those rare individuals who can subordinate her ego to another's during a séance and genuinely cooperate to produce a fruitful session. Modestly Ruth maintains that her own abilities are still in the development stage, and she insists that she is content to work in the shadow of a master such as Olof Jonsson, the sensitive who participated in the famous Moon-to-Earth ESP experiment with astronaut Ed Mitchell.

"Ruth is very good," Olof said of his friend. "She gives excellent readings and has produced ectoplasm and a wide variety of manifestations during séances. One day I know that she will become very famous as a medium."

Betty Jonsson, Olof's wife, and Ingrid Bergstrom have

the following tale to tell of one night's séance with Olof that produced so much anxiety and left such vivid memories that they remember it as if it happened yesterday.

"I will tell you about a séance no one will believe," said Ingrid Bergstrom. "Betty attended it just before she married Olof, and she became so frightened that afterward I asked her if she would still go through with the wedding."

"I was so frightened that I was actually crying," Betty Jonsson agreed.

"It was held at Verdandi's, in our spooky room," stated Ingrid. "That's where they used to have the slot machines in the days when the clubs could have gambling. And there's still quite an atmosphere in there, I tell you. We used it as a storeroom for tables and silverware and things we weren't using.

"We had the lights dimmed but not completely off. Betty held Olof's right hand and I held his left hand, and we had our feet on his feet so that he could not move. I think we sat for half an hour before something happened."

"You were singing a little bit, remember?" added Betty.

"Yes," Ingrid agreed. "And then we heard footsteps, like dancing. Like someone dancing a waltz. Then the steps came from all over. A cloth came off a table without disturbing a tray of glasses sitting on it and came whisking by my face. I had an awful, cold feeling."

"Then a glass came flying through the air," Betty noted.

"And for anybody to have reached those glasses, he would have had to go stepping over stacked-up chairs and tables. But that glass just came floating off a tray," said Ingrid.

"You could hear things flying through the room, and footsteps running around. I had always enjoyed attending séances, but this was the first time that I had ever been afraid. Since we were the only three people in the room,

GHOSTS AMONG US

who was throwing things all over the place?" asked Betty.

"The heavy table at which we were sitting rose up, and another table that was sitting on top of another across the room did the same and crashed to the floor," Ingrid explained.

This was not the only scary séance Ingrid attended with the Jonssons. She told the following story about a particular Valentine's Day séance in her home.

"*Ja*, my cousin from Detroit and her husband wanted to meet Betty and Olof. My cousin's husband had made up his mind that he was not going to believe anything that happened that night, and he still says that if he had not seen those things with his own eyes, he never would have believed it. Now, he says, he sits at his job and wonders about the meaning of it all.

"We had dinner and afterward placed our hands on the dining-room table. It is made of teak and is very big. It must weigh over two hundred pounds. But all of a sudden it began to rise and bang itself to the floor. After a while a young couple, who was having a party below us, knocked on the door and asked if I were trying to tell them that they were disturbing us. 'Oh, no,' I told them, 'it's just my table. Olof Jonsson is here, and we are making the table walk by itself.'

"One of the table legs actually broke. Who would have thought such heavy wood could shatter? But it raised itself high and slammed itself down hard many times, as if it were angry.

"I remember once moving out of its way, because it was coming after me. And it nearly got my cousin's husband into a corner. He, too, wondered if it were angry at him.

"It was strange because we sat at first with our hands lightly touching the table. When it started to move, I looked to see if anybody was trying to move it with their hands, but then everybody had their hands above the table.

"Olof was standing away from the table. He had been sitting for just a little while at the very beginning of the séance, but soon he rose to stand in a corner of the room.

"When the table began to jump, everybody moved away. That heavy table jumped like a horse, and everybody backed away from it. It was like a living thing."

A Ghost Tour of Haunted Chicago

Richard T. Crowe takes the brave and fearless on a guided trip through Chicago's most haunted sites. Here is his account of his years on the ghost trail.

"I've been interested in ghostly and spontaneous phenomena in Chicago since my high-school days. When I was working on my master's degree in English at DePaul University, I became very friendly with Dr. Houck, head of the geography department.

"Dr. Houck was always running some sort of tour or other for the geographical society at the university, and he asked me if haunted places might not lend themselves to a tour. I had never thought of that angle before. I plotted out a route for what was intended to be a onetime tour for Halloween 1973. There was some local press on it, and we ended up turning away over two hundred people. I got a list of those who were denied the first tour and offered them tours of their own. From that point I just never stopped. I run the tour an average of five times a month, except in October, which hits ten or twelve times before Halloween.

"For the most part I have chosen places where paranormal phenomena has reoccurred over the years. The sites range from cemeteries to churches to street corners. Because of the large size of the groups, we are limited to either public or semipublic places.

"A very unusual thing happened on the first tour. Cindy Graham, who works in placement at DePaul, is a bit of a camera bug. She was taking slides, and when her slide of the statue of Our Lady of Perpetual Help at Holy Family Church was developed, mysterious faces appeared behind the statue.

"We went to investigate, and sure enough, there were these mysterious images right in the plaster. The paper over the plaster is peeled, and these 'faces' show through. Depending on where you stand and how the lighting is, you can make out a few too many faces.

"In 1923, an extremely large book was published to commemorate the history of Holy Family. The church was built as a Jesuit parish in 1857, and the Jesuits are very good at documentation. Because of the detailed information in this book, we know exactly when everything was painted, where the statues come from—the whole history of the church. We know that there were *never* any faces painted on that wall. It was just that chance photograph that brought them out. No one knows how long they may have been there.

"Holy Family Church, by the way, was built over running water, the Red Creek, and the site of an old Indian battlefield. During the Great Fire of Chicago the church was saved, according to the people of the time, by the divine intervention of Our Lady of Perpetual Help.

"The statue of the Blessed Mother stands in a niche at the front of the church and hasn't been moved in well over a hundred years. It weighs about eight hundred pounds, and in addition to the mysterious faces there is a crack that runs the full length of the church from top to bottom, which is also credited to the divine intervention of Our Lady of Perpetual Help.

"Several people have experienced something at the grave of Mary Alice Quinn, who has been nicknamed Chicago's Miracle Child and was buried in Holy Sepulchre Cemetery in 1935. She was a small Irish-American girl, very mystically inclined, who nearly is the Chicago version of Saint Theresa, the Little Flower, to whom Mary Alice was very devoted. Before she died, Mary Alice told her parents that she wanted to help people. Many incidents have been related, especially in the late 1930s and 1940s, of Mary Alice Quinn appearing to people throughout Chicago's South Side.

"She has also appeared to people around the world! Her grave site has become a pilgrimage spot. The "pilgrims" come to the cemetery, pray, and leave candles at her grave. Many people take away handfuls of soil.

"The manifestation that is most often reported at the grave site is the overwhelming scent of roses, even though there are no flowers there," Richard Crowe explained. "During my tours people have been overcome by the scent. The aroma has become so strong that people have to walk away from the site to catch their breath.

"I generally have about forty-five people on a bus, and when I take count of those who have smelled the roses, there are usually in the vicinity of fifteen people who raise their hands.

"The scent seems to be more noticeable in the winter months than any other time of year. Again, there may be a psychological factor involved here. Because of the cold weather and everyone realizing that there should not be flowers around, people may instantly recognize that there is something unusual happening when they catch the scent of roses.

"At Saint Rita's Church—which became very famous on All Souls' Day, 1960, when several witnesses saw phantom monks in the church—many people on the tour have claimed to have heard the organ playing by itself. According to some of the parishioners I have contacted, the organ played by itself when the phantom monks were seen.

"We visit a good number of churches on the tour, since, due to urban renewal, haunted houses don't last long! Once they're deserted, they're soon cleared away. I have to concentrate the tours on the more permanent buildings.

"We also have a number of phantom hitchhikers. We have a beautiful Jewish girl who has black hair and dresses in the flapper-style clothing of the 1920s.

"We know she's Jewish because she disappears in a Jewish cemetery, Jewish Waldheim. She has been seen to walk into a mausoleum and vanish. She's been sighted a number of times.

"We also have a young Mexican girl who appears between Cline and Cudahy Avenues, just outside of Gary, Indiana. This phantom was picked up by a cabdriver in 1965 and dematerialized in his car.

"To me the most fascinating phantom hitchhiker is the one called Resurrection Mary, a beautiful, blond Polish girl. We have very ethnically inclined ghosts in Chicago.

"Mary was buried in Resurrection Cemetery, which is where she gets her nickname, on Archer Avenue on the South Side of Chicago. Archer, by the way, has hauntings running the entire length of the avenue. It was built over an old Indian trail. So many things have happened over that old path that I think it must be like a ley line (a prehistoric system of aligning sacred power sites).

"During the 1930s and 1940s, Mary was often picked up at dances by various people. She would ask for a ride toward Resurrection Cemetery, down by Archer, saying that she lived down that way.

"As people drove her home she would yell at them to stop the car in front of the cemetery gates. She would get out of the car, run across the road, and dematerialize at the gates.

"Resurrection Mary was also seen just before Christmas, dancing down the street, down Archer, east of Harlem Avenue.

"Two young fellows who saw her were instantly aware that there was something very unusual taking place," Crowe continued. "They stood and watched this girl dance by them, and they both got the strangest sensation. There were other people walking by who didn't even notice the girl. The fellows ran home and told their father what they had seen. They'd never heard of Resurrection Mary, but their father recognized her by the description they provided. I investigated and found out that a week before this sighting, Mary had been seen dancing around the cemetery's fence.

"I have at least seven first-person accounts of people who have had Mary open their car doors and jump in, but this is the first first-person account I have of someone who met her at a dance and took her home.

"I quote from the report: 'She sat in the front with the driver and me. When we approached the front gate at Resurrection Cemetery, she asked to stop and get out. It was a few minutes before midnight.

"'We said, 'You can't possibly live here.'

"'She said, 'I know, but I have to get out.'

"'So being a gentleman, and she being so beautiful, I didn't want to create a disturbance. I got out, and she got out without saying anything.

"'It was dark. She crossed the road, running, and as she approached the gate, she disappeared.

"'I already had her name and address, so early Monday

morning, all three of us came to the number and street in the stockyards area. We climbed the front steps to her home. We rang and knocked on the door. The mother opened the door, and lo and behold, the girl's color picture was on the piano, looking right at us. The mother said she was dead. We told her our story and left.

" 'My friends and I did not pursue the matter any more, and we haven't seen her again. All three of us went into the service thereafter and lost contact with each other.'

"My particular area of interest in psychical research lies in the area of spontaneous phenomena, and there is so much more concentrated here in Chicago than I have found in any other area.

"I think possibly part of the reason for this is due to the ethnic makeup of Chicago. I have mentioned that many of the ghosts that I have come across are ethnically oriented. We do have strong ethnic communities in Chicago, and these ghosts seem to be a part of the folk consciousness of these people.

"In Chicago we have Old World traditions and their adaptation to the American way of life. We have the grafted folkways of the past, and we have a brand-new type of developing folklore, both functioning at the same time.

"Chicago might be some kind of power place, with the ley lines leading to it and emanating from it. Archer Avenue, among other places, was built on an old Indian trail. Saint James Church, also on Archer, was built on the site of a French signal fort that dates back to the 1700s. Before that, the site served an Indian settlement.

"Many of these haunted churches, either consciously or unconsciously, may have been erected over American Indian medicine-power places.

"Chicago is also near the Continental Divide, which is the portage that serves as the link between the Great Lakes system and the Mississippi River system. It is a natural halfway point between these two geological and geographical areas. We do have a number of these power places, or 'window areas,' in the city, and I want to keep hearing from people who have had various experiences there."

• 10 •

Haunted Ground

As the reader has by now perceived, so-called "haunted ground" may exist anywhere—from beside a quiet mountain stream to a rest room in a busy bus terminal in a major metropolitan area. In fact, the larger the city, the more likely one is to encounter the ghosts of murder victims or others who died unexpectedly.

According to one school of thought, these people were denied the time to make peace with themselves when they died or they have left unresolved emotional attachments that prevent their spirits from leaving earth.

Ian Currie, a sociologist at the University of Guelph in Ontario, Canada, remarked to journalist Franklin R. Ruehl that "the larger the city, the larger its population of ghosts. This is in direct proportion to the higher death rates from crimes and accidents in the big cities."

Psychic-sensitive Shawn Robbins states that ghosts tend to linger at the site of their death. "For example," she explained, "if they were shot to death in an alley, their ghosts will remain in that alley. People who die in their apartments are likely to haunt the subsequent tenants."

Ms. Robbins said that there may be certain "signs" that can indicate the presence of a ghost—clammy hands, a cold sweat, dry mouth and throat, a feeling of impending doom, rapid heartbeat, and possibly a musty smell. She quickly adds, however, that one should not panic if one encounters a ghost.

"These ghosts pose no actual threat to you. They're just disturbed souls who became entrapped in a situation beyond their control."

A Ghostly Cottage in Dearborn, Michigan

Joyce Hagelthorn of the *Dearborn Press* brought the following account to light in her May 10, 1973, column "I've Never Told Anyone But . . ."

Laura Jean Daniels was walking home from work late one night. She remembers looking up at the moon, reflecting briefly about how it must have affected the astronauts to look back at Earth from it. When she lowered her eyes, the street before her was no longer familiar.

"The pavement on the sidewalk was gone, and I was walking on a brick path. There were no houses on either side of me, but several hundred feet before me was a thatched roof and cottage. And there was a heavy scent of roses and honeysuckle in the air," Ms. Daniels told Joyce Hagelthorn.

The bewildered woman continued to walk on, desperately fighting panic.

"As I walked up the brick path and drew closer to the cottage, I could see that there were two people sitting in the garden . . . a man and a young woman . . . in very old-fashioned clothes. They were obviously in love, for they were embracing, and as I drew closer I could see the expression on the girl's face . . . and believe me, she was in love."

Just as Laura Jean Daniels was wondering if she should cough or somehow signal her intrusion into such a private moment, a small dog came running out from under a bush and began barking.

"He was quivering all over. The man looked up and called to the dog to stop barking, and asked him what he was barking at. I somehow realized that he couldn't see me. And yet, I could smell the flowers and feel the gate beneath my hand.

"While I was trying to make up my mind what to do, I turned to look back at the way I had just come . . . and there was my street! But I could still feel the gate in my hand, and yet, as I turned once again toward the cottage, it was gone. I was standing right in the middle of my own block, just a few doors from my home. The cottage, the lovers, and the wee dog . . . were gone."

Joyce Hagelthorn is a woman who has been "tuned in" for a number of years. Mrs. Hagelthorn has spent a great deal of time exploring our plastic reality; consequently she is well aware that many men and women have had experiences similar to that of Laura Jean Daniels.

"Did Laura Jean project herself into the past?" she asked. "Would an observer on Laura Jean's street have been able to see and talk with her while she was visiting the cottage? Or did Laura Jean step briefly into another dimension?"

Bill Freitag, of Aurora, Illinois, told me of the time that he stayed overnight in a haunted house on a dare from his fraternity brothers. He had been about to write the whole thing off as the dullest night in his life when he heard noises in the front hallway. He stepped away from his "nest" in a front room to confront the image of a man in a belted smoking jacket about to mount the staircase.

The man seemed as startled as Bill, but both of them kept their cool. The man continued on his way up the staircase, then stopped near the top, slowly turning around to look down at Bill. Their eyes met for several seconds, then the man resumed his movement up the stairs and walked through a wall.

When Bill told me that he later learned there had once been a doorway to a bedroom at the very spot where the "ghost" had walked through the wall, I told him that he may not have confronted a ghost at all.

In my opinion, ghosts have a very automatic nature: They do the same things at the same time on each occasion, activated by something in the psychic atmosphere. I have often used the analogy that a ghost is very much like a strip of film that is replayed whenever someone of the properly sympathetic psychic affinity is there to serve as the "receiving set" or the "projector."

I suggested that Bill may have briefly stepped into another era in the dimension of time, and that he had entered that house—circa the turn of the century, judging by Bill's detailed description of the ghost's clothing—at a time when the paterfamilias was preparing to retire. The gentleman in another era also saw a "ghost" when he encountered the wraith of a tall, thin youth with shoulder-length hair and a beard.

Strange Knockings in a Depot of the Underground Railroad

The heavy shadows in the eerie, cluttered subbasement closed around us like dark, living things made curious by our invasion of their dismal domain.

GHOSTS AMONG US

"Do you feel something moving under your foot?" Irene Hughes, the famous psychic-sensitive, asked in a sudden whisper. "The ground seems to be vibrating."

Joan Hurling, a reporter who accompanied us on our "psychic safari," stepped closer to Mrs. Hughes. "Hold your foot next to mine and see if you can feel the vibration," the Chicago seeress bade the journalist. "Can you feel it?"

The three of us had ventured into the darkened subbasement in the old home in Clinton, Iowa, while the remainder of our party stayed outside. The house, now owned by a couple we shall call the Whites, is said to be one of the oldest homes in the historic city. An old lumber town where some of the wealthiest timber barons in the United States lived, Clinton, maintained many of the ancient mansions that give silent, but impressive, testimony to a once colorful past. This particular home, in which we now rummaged around in the dark, had a specific bit of history that we were waiting for Irene to determine through her psychic impressions.

"I get an impression of a stream, a stream . . . a river," Irene said, struggling with the influx of psychic half-thoughts, images impressions, and symbols. "There was a passage that went to a river."

I thrust the flashlight's beam around the cool, rank blackness stabbing the close, inquiring shadows with a sword of illumination. Irene closed her eyes.

"I feel—" She stopped, the image obviously puzzling her. "Why would there be a stream of people going through here? I almost feel like these people are prisoners or something. Slaves? I see slaves, black slaves, streaming through this place."

Irene was correct. The subbasement of the old home had been used as a way station on the Underground Railroad during the Civil War. Her psychic receiving apparatus had been properly tuned in. She had seen slaves streaming through the subbasement, entering a tunnel that would lead them to another depot on the "railroad" to freedom. And according to what few available records exist, there had been a small stream that had at one time flowed through the tunnel. A decaying well in a corner of the basement indicated that the stream may have been used as a source of water for the house's inhabitants.

Why the necessity for such secrecy in aiding escaping slaves in the far North Yankee city of Clinton, Iowa?

Iowa may have fought strenuously on the Union side in the Civil War (so strenuously, in fact, that the state lost more young men as a result of the Civil War than in any other war), but Clinton—with its wealthy timber barons, its prosperous trade with the South, and its many investments in Southern plantations—was pro-Confederacy. In this Mississippi river town one could get oneself tarred and feathered for speaking out against slavery—and many of the early abolitionists met precisely that fate in Clinton.

Audible Manifestations

Although Irene's on-target hit of the old subbasement's history would have been impressive enough for that evening's experiment, her psychic power would soon activate a series of audible manifestations that would provide an additional psychic treat for our party of investigators.

After we had come from the darkened subbasement to the attractively decorated finished basement, Irene asked the owner of the house, Mrs. White, if she had ever heard somebody whistling in the house when she was alone. Our hostess answered no, and Irene frowned her puzzlement, commenting that she *saw* an old man who liked to whittle and whistle.

GHOSTS AMONG US

When someone asked Irene if she felt that the house had always looked as it did at the present time, she replied, "I feel as though there was once a little shedlike area that was on this end out here."

"Yes, that's right. There was a porch," Mrs. White agreed. "The four-by-fours are still visible on the outside. They've sawed them off, but you can see—"

"Was there also another little house out there?" Irene inquired.

"Not that I know of, but there is a little walk out there," Mrs. White replied.

Irene then asked, "Are you thinking of digging up an apple tree?"

Mrs. White surprisingly answered yes. "We were thinking of cutting down the one out front."

"I see a cardinal sitting in this tree," Irene exclaimed.

"There's one out there that wakes us up every morning!"

"I hear the name Baker," Irene said, closing her eyes and swaying a bit unsteadily. "With that name I feel like I want to go into a trance."

It was at this moment that everyone assembled heard a series of knocks sounding from somewhere upstairs. Writer Warren Smith ran upstairs to investigate, but he found nothing or no one that might have been responsible for the loud raps. We immediately played back the tape recorders and were elated to find that the cassettes had clearly picked up the unexplained knockings.

With Irene Hughes in a light trance and acting as a kind of psychic bloodhound, the party found itself upstairs in a room that the sensitive associated with the name Baker. When the medium had situated herself "just so" in the room, we once again heard a knocking—but much softer than before.

"Phew, it's knocking under me," Irene exclaimed.

"I also felt the vibrations." Mrs. Hughes and I stood alone in the room, while the other members of the party were crowded around the doorway.

"It stopped," Irene noted. "It was like someone was knocking under my feet, and when I moved over here, it did it again."

"Before we came upstairs," Glenn McWane, another party member said, "the knocking seemed to be coming from this door"—he indicated the front door—"but just a little while ago it seemed to be coming from that room."

"Just as soon as you said the name Baker, the pounding started," Mrs. White added.

"Well, if Mr. Baker is here, please come up. We want to see you and talk to you," insisted Irene.

The Appearance of a Glowing Luminescence

Irene said that she could hear soft whisperings, and since she seemed to be slipping once more into light trance, she was helped to a sofa and permitted to sit back in a comfortable position. She seemed at once to witness a rapid montage of historical scenes from Old Clinton, and she mentioned a number of important names, which various people in the room recognized.

A very pale, glowing luminescence appeared on the wall just to the right of Irene's head, and certain members of the group said that they heard the knocking sound again.

Although Irene continued to bring forth an enormous amount of material that night, the great majority of the names and events were simply uncheckable. The abstract of the house only went back to 1889, but the home is thought to be at least one hundred and twenty years old. Any of the names of men and women that Irene gave may have had a dramatic or transient role in the history of the quaint old place, but there exists no way to prove the validity of these ostensibly psychic recalls. She tuned in several times during the evening on scenes and characters that may very well have had an importance to the functioning of the Underground Railroad. But since the operation of the Freedom Train had to be conducted with the utmost secrecy in Clinton circa 1860, only the scantest records remain.

In terms of a dramatic hit, however, Irene did most certainly identify the home as having once been a way station on the Underground Railroad. And for the benefit of those of us who were assembled in the Whites' home that evening, someone or something did noisily respond to the name Baker.

Blood and Emotions—Can They Saturate the Environment?

In his article "Battles and Ghosts" (*Prediction* magazine, July 1952), John Pendragon tried to show that in regard to England, the eastern part of the country produces the greatest crop of haunted sites. The late, eminent British seer stated that such might be due to the fact that the eastern area of England has been the scene of most of England's battles—especially battles to stave off invasion. Pendragon also made reference to the theory that the districts may, in some unknown way, have become "sensitized" as the result of these emotional conflicts involving bloodshed.

It has for some time been concluded that great human emotion can saturate a place or an object with its own particular vibration. On that assumption, is it not possible—or even probable—that the scenes of the bloody conflicts have, so to speak, "sensitized" the very soil upon which they took place?

Many readers may be living in a house that is built on the site of an early battle, recorded or unrecorded, or even the scene of a human sacrifice or a terrible murder. Perhaps you smile indulgently, but such a case is by no means impossible. Many a sedate parlor may be standing on a place that has witnessed the most grim and terrifying scenes.

If places are thus sensitized, is it not possible that the original cause of the sensitization does not always manifest as a tangible haunting at all? But a place so emotionally saturated holds certain unknown qualities that are necessary for the production of a later haunt that arises from a completely different event.

Granted, hauntings frequently *seem* to be manifestations of a long-ago event. Yet the haunting that manifests to us may only do so because the site has been previously conditioned by an earlier emotional event. The first event, a battle or some occurrence highly charged with emotions, may never manifest to our eyes and ears at all, yet the second event, which happens on the same site, *does* manifest.

In short, it is the second event that "lights up" like a "light bulb" that has been plugged into the "socket" after the current has been switched on. It lights up but would not have done so had there been no current available. In the same way, such sensitization may depend upon the nature of the subsoil.

John Pendragon stated that eastern England is an especially haunted area, and its geological composition is composed mainly of soil types of the Tertiary and Quanternary Periods, the most recent eras of geological history. The Tertiary Period of rock includes marine limestone, London clay, shelly sands, and gravels. In the Quanternary Period one finds peat, alluvium, silt, mud, loam, and sometimes gravel.

Essex probably contains the greatest number of haunted sites, and Essex is eighty percent London Clay, the remainder mostly chalk. This particular county and its clay subsoil may provide a key to the problem of why certain areas are more haunted than others. The question is: Are certain subsoils more sensitized than others?

Millikan, the astrophysicist, discovered that certain soils absorb cosmic waves more readily than others, some soils acting as conductors and others as insulators. The French physicist Lahkovsky noted that the highest incidence of cancer appeared to occur on clay soils and soils rich in ores, and that the lowest incidence was to be found where the soil was sand or gravel. Lahkovsky attributed this fact to the deflection of cosmic waves by the conducting soils, causing an imbalance in body cells, which, he maintained, are miniature oscillating circuits. Therefore we may deduce that cosmic rays or the deflection of them by a soil predominantly of clay does, in some way yet unknown to us, act as an aid to the production of phenomena that we call haunting by spirits.

It would seem that the clays, chalk, and alluvial soils are more sensitized than the ancient rocks, such as granite, gneiss, coal, old red sandstone, limestone, and so forth. Perhaps clay has the property of storing or deflecting the X energy while granite and basalt do not. Subterranean water may play a part. We might also point out that the most haunted places in England are on the "drier side" of the country. Pendragon was convinced that the reason why some areas are more haunted than others lies in a fusion of a number of factors, widely different, but that the geology of the district is one of them.

"Placebound" ghosts and haunts appear periodically in the same settings and perform the same actions time after time, as if a bit of ethereal motion-picture film were being projected on something. Such manifestations constitute only one kind of ghost.

"I believe there is evidence to show that the earthly dead have communicated with the earthly living without the aid of a spirit medium as a go-between," Pendragon said. "I think there is plenty of evidence to show that thoughts have a wave length and that these waves are capable of being sensed by the discarnate. Such thought-waves would, of course, include the thoughts that constitute what we call remembrance, especially if there be a spiritual and emotional bond between the living and the dead. There are many recorded instances where discarnate personalities have manifested to the living in times of danger to the latter—and on other occasions, too. Certainly the materialization of my grandfathers and my mother have provided me with the most convincing personal proof of such communication."

A Cackling Hag With an Evil Grin

Miss H. V. brought Pendragon an interesting case that may serve to illustrate one kind of haunting.

One winter evening, just as Miss H. V. and her mother were about to sit down to tea in their old house in South London, they heard a strange snapping noise in the room, like dry sticks burning. At the same time they both became aware of a vile smell that seemed to permeate the room.

"Look!" her mother shouted, and Miss H. V. followed

the thrust of her pointing, trembling forefinger to a corner of the room. There she saw a small, wizened old woman with a shawl over her head. She was grinning evilly and cackling at them.

Miss H. V.'s mother fell to the floor in a faint. "I was absolutely speechless with fright," Miss H. V. admitted, "but I somehow found the strength to pick up the teapot, which was full of scalding tea, and hurl it at the old woman.

"The teapot passed through the hag and smashed to steaming bits against the wall. The ugly creature seemed not to notice my attack. She just kept on staring at me and cackling at her own evil and private joke.

"Then a most extraordinary thing happened. It seemed as if all the energy was being sucked out of my body by the old woman. I guess that I must have passed out, too.

"When Mother and I regained consciousness, the hag had vanished. We had nothing to show for our experience but the broken teapot and a pool of tea. Somehow, though, we felt we had been very lucky."

Miss H. V. paused to light the cigarette with which she had been toying ever since she had sat down, then asked the question that had been troubling her. "Tell me, Mr. Pendagon, do you think that we have a ghost?"

The psychic-sensitive replied that he would reserve comment until he had seen the situation from a psychic viewpoint. He wrote her name and address on a sheet of paper and concentrated on it. An image came, but it was terribly distorted and made no sense.

As Pendagon often told me, he did not get wrong impressions. Either an image comes or it does not, but he did not get jumbled pictures.

"I abandoned the slip of paper and turned to my large map of London," he said. "Perhaps a bit of map dousing would set the matter straight. I located the tiny dot that represented Miss H. V.'s home and placed my finger upon it. Once again I received nothing but a blur of mental images."

"Is something wrong?" Miss H. V. asked solicitously, sensing his acute sense of frustration.

Pendragon felt that something was different rather than wrong, and he was determined to learn why he had experienced such a queer blockage. Once more he looked at the map of London.

"I was about to place my finger on Miss H. V.'s home for another try when a tiny bell rang somewhere in my subconscious. I stepped quickly away from the map and walked to a section of my crowded bookshelves. I selected the book that I was after, paged rapidly to the proper heading, and within a few moments I had a most important part of the answer.

"I believe strongly that the site of a haunted house is very important," he said to Miss H. V. "It so happens that your home was built on the site of a once famous mental hospital. No wonder I was getting only jumbled images. What else might one expect from the insane?"

Miss H. V. became very upset. "Mother and I are to be roommates with an insane ghost?"

"You may never see the ghost again," Pendragon said. "I get that your old woman is a placebound phantom, a former inmate of the asylum who, in her rational moments, deeply resented being put in a mental hospital. There is no haunting in the sense that a spirit has returned to try to put some matter right or to issue a warning. You saw an emotion-charged scene from the past that somehow was retained in the sensitized physical properties of the old hospital site."

A Phantom Monk

The open-minded, scholarly sensitive Pendragon was the first to admit that theories of hauntings overlap one another, and he certainly stood firmly against any kind of dogma when it came to explaining matters of the unseen world. Just as an ancient site may be sensitized with the mechanical and repetitious playback of a phantom highwayman or a cackling hag, so may the saturated edifice help to retain the earthbound spirit of one who returns to seek help in putting some long-forgotten matter right within himself.

Once, when calling on a friend who lived in Lincoln, Pendragon was very much interested to hear that a few nights before he had seen a ghost.

"I was lying fully awake in bed in the early hours of the morning," his friend said. "I happened to glance at the doorway and observed a figure dressed in a monk's brown habit. It was holding out its hands toward me, as if in supplication, but under its hood there was no face, only a dark space."

Pendragon's friend had reacted in a manner that hardly would be unusual under the circumstances. He shouted at the ghost in a loud voice and told it to go away. At the sound of this command, the figure vanished.

"It was at this point that my old dog began to howl and bark," he said. "When at last I managed to force myself out of bed, I found old Hector shivering and trembling. Now, John, tell me about what I saw. How could it have been a ghost? Why, my house is only a few years old. There haven't been any murders or scenes of violence or even any natural deaths in this house."

"Perhaps not," Pendagon told him, "but the psychic atmosphere is very highly charged in this area. First of all, I get that your house is standing on the site of a monastery. (This fact was later established by reference to earlier maps of the district.) Secondly, I get that you saw the earthbound spirit of a monk, who was appealing to you to help him. The fact that you could not see his face, but only a dark space, may have been the spiritual symbol of an earthly fear or fixation that was binding him to earth. What a pity you said 'Get away!' You should have said, 'In the name of the Father, Son, and Holy Ghost, what do you want?'"

"Are you kidding me, John?" his friend asked. "I certainly don't want to make myself available for the confessions of ghostly monks. And what do I do if the phantom reappears some night?"

"That is very unlikely," Pendragon said. "You have ordered it away, so it probably will not appear again as long as you are living in this house."

"That is very good news indeed." He grinned.

"It is a pity, though," the psychic remarked. "Imagine that poor spirit wandering in a type of limbo for generations. I have an idea. I know an excellent medium who could—"

"Oh, no, you don't, John!" his friend warned him. "There'll be no séances in my house. I'm not running a clinic for troubled ghosts!"

· 11 ·

Ethereal Advisers and Ghostly Guides

"Certain things happened to me when alone in my room which convinced me that there are spiritual intelligences that can warn us and advise us." Who made this statement? A crackpot? Someone hoodwinked by a phony spirit medium?

The man who said these words was none of these. In fact, he won the Nobel prize for literature in 1923; wrote thirty-five books of poetry, plays, essays, and criticism; organized the Irish Literary Society of London and Dublin; founded the Irish Literary Theater; and was a senator from the Irish Free State.

William Butler Yeats has often been unfairly criticized as being dream-headed and absentminded, but the list of things that he accomplished during his productive life shows the lack of truth in such criticism. Yeats's desire to be a whole man led him down the mysterious path of the mystic and brought him into contact with the most noted Spiritualists and psychics of his day.

Even from childhood Yeats had a great interest in the imaginative world of the occult. His mother told him fairy tales and folk tales, while his father, a pre-Raphaelite painter, gave him an education befitting an artist. His stimulated imagination led him to study the occult under a man named George Russell in Dublin.

While still a young man, Yeats and some friends formed the Dublin Hermetic Society, and Russell's house became a meeting place for many young imaginative thinkers, philosophers, and visionaries, all sharing Yeats's interest in the power of symbolism in man's life.

Yeats had a favorite uncle who was a strong believer in the supernatural. Together they would share visions when Yeats came to visit.

Once, when the uncle was taken sick with a fever, Yeats was able to soothe him simply by thinking of water (a symbol).

The doctor, who looked in on the uncle, was surprised to find him resting easily. When Yeats explained what he had done, the doctor passed it off as simply a form of hypnotism.

A Vision via Invocation to the Moon

The psychic side of Yeats's life had a great influence on the work that eventually won him the Nobel prize for literature. On one occasion he made an invocation to the moon for seven nights in succession. He was finally rewarded with a vision of a centaur and a woman shooting at a star.

Perhaps this could have been passed off as the construction of a weary mind after so long a vigil, but people all over the area, some of them friends of Yeats, reported seeing the apparition at the same time. This particular incident appeared in Yeats's poetry many times and in the poetry of such friends as Arthur Symons.

Yeats was convinced that great truths could be learned from the spiritual side of man—truths which, in fact, could not be comprehended in any other manner. To this end he investigated the spirit world of the magician and seer, hoping to understand more clearly the value and power of the symbol over men.

Automatic Writing

Shortly after he married in 1917, Yeats and his wife began experimenting with automatic writing. To their surprise Mrs. Yeats was extremely successful with this form of "spirit" communication, and Yeats filled many notebooks with the messages that came to his wife.

While on a lecture tour in California, Yeats found that the spirit guide that was giving his wife advice through automatic writing would also answer questions through the voice of Mrs. Yeats while she lay asleep. This proved a great asset in Yeats's investigation of the spirit world, as the automatic writing was physically exhausting for his wife. Yeats identified his spirit guide as Leo Africanus, who was actually a sixteenth-century traveler, poet, and geographer.

This spirit direction came accompanied by strange sounds and peculiar, unexplainable odors. Sometimes the odor was of snuffed candles and, at other times, of the thick smell of flowers.

Although Yeats put great value on the Spiritualistic side of man, he trusted no medium completely, except his wife. He remained constantly skeptical of the words of the professional mediums, realizing the hit-and-miss nature of their insights. Yeats sought truth above all else.

Yeats's verse could not help but be affected by his dabbling in the occult, and the imagery of his poetry is strongly influenced by the experiences he shared with the uncharted world of the paranormal.

Encountering a "Conveyor" From Beyond

The late British seer John Pendragon shared the following account of a series of visitations from an ethereal adviser, a spirit guide.

"It was in April 1944, while writing at a large table pushed into a bay window of the biggest room in the house, that I suddenly felt I was not alone, although there was no other person on the premises and would not be until evening.

"I felt that there was a person standing behind me watching my actions, but I saw nobody. I knew that I should, if possible, keep relaxed and quiet, and it was not long before I picked up a clairvoyant impression of the personality of a man in the room. He apparently knew that I had sensed his presence, and I began rapidly to 'see' him.

"He appeared to be about sixty years of age. Gray-headed, neat, and tiny in appearance, he wore a suit of a delicate checkered pattern and radiated a spirit of goodwill and friendliness. Immediately I made an effort to communicate with him telepathically.

"'Who are you and why are you here?' I flashed.

"'My name is not important. I am here because it is my work to act on the instructions of others in regard to yourself.'

"'That seems a little puzzling.' I said, communicating telepathically. 'What is the nature of your work in regard to me?'

"'I don't think that you would understand the nature of my work, because it relates to matters and conditions that are outside the comprehension of your world, but let us say

GHOSTS AMONG US

that I bring a kind of psychic power to you. I am conveyer of a power that comes from my world. This power has to pass through me from its source. Actually, although I am a conveyer, I know very little about the power and the way it operates. I leave these things to friends of mine who understand, and I accept their words and their instructions.'

" 'Is it the power of God?'

" 'In a sense, yes, because all powers stem from God.'

" 'But why should this power be directed at me?'

" 'You will see later.'

"I felt that I could not get much technical information from him at this stage, so I turned to more personal matters.

" 'When did you die? That is, when did you pass from an earth life?'

" 'In the period of earth time that was called 1912.'

" 'What was your work while you were here?'

" 'I was a gentleman's personal servant and valet.'

" 'Were you interested in psychic matters?'

" 'No. Although I believed that we survived the earthly body, I made no study of the matter. The subject was too profound for me. I know a little more now, but I still find it profound, and I prefer to let others take the lead. I am content to do as instructed, and that makes me feel happy. Happiness and affinity play big parts in my world.'

" 'Have you been with me before?'

" 'Yes, many times. But you have not been consciously aware of me each time to the degree that you are at this moment.'

"It has to be realized that although I am expressing these communications in words, we simply flashed thoughts one to the other. Words are the tools I must use to convey what we flashed. In half a second I could get and send what I have needed minutes to write or to speak in words.

" 'Do you see both my future and past?'

"'In what you would call an outline, yes.'

"'Then what is my future?'

"'I am not permitted to make revelations to you about your future in your world. You must accept that there are good reasons for this. I have to obey my instructions. I am happy to do so, for by so doing, I serve. When I was in your world, I was happy to serve in a very small way. That is one of the reasons why I was chosen for my present work.'

"'Do you retain memory of your earth life?'

"'I do.'

"'Does everybody in your world retain memory of earth life?'

"'It is necessary for them to do so. There can be many reasons why this might be necessary.'"

"Born" Into the Ethereal World

"I asked him numerous questions, but for the most part, either he did not choose to reply or he did not have the knowledge. As he pointed out, just as vast numbers of people on earth do not know how much natural phenomena 'works'—such as biology, psychology, astronomy. Thus was the case in his world. Just as one had to be born into an earth world, so one had to be 'born' into an etheric world.

"He telepathized that there were many conditions in the etheric world that were far beyond his ken, and certainly would be beyond mine, and that spirit and intellect were not one and the same thing. Many of my queries were answered with, 'You'll know later.'

"Sometimes the contact was sharp, but at other times— for he visited me on many occasions—it was difficult. I attributed this to my own thoughts and emotions creating a jamming of some kind.

"I tried to get his earth surname and, after several trials, clairvoyantly saw a symbol of a fox. I thereby assumed that his name was, or had been, Fox. He communicated telepathically that names mattered little but personality mattered much, and that it was by personality that identification was established in the afterlife.

"After a number of visits he announced that he would not be coming again, as 'My work is finished with you now.' He added that I might be conscious of some 'friends' after his departure. He gave me his blessing and I was conscious of him no more, although he did return once again some years later.

"A few days later, again while sitting typing, I had a further clairvoyant impression of four etheric personalities—two men and two women. One woman was Chinese. (The accuracy of this statement regarding a Chinese 'guide,' if guide she was, was later confirmed by Mrs. Moira Wilson Vawser, a well-known medium.) The second woman I could not get so clearly, but it seemed to me that she was engaged in recording the meeting, like a stenographer. Of the two men, one was a doctor. The other I could not place, but he impressed me that in earth life he had been a magistrate.

"Strangely, this little group seemed to be part of a larger one—hundreds of people—'beyond' them, as if the four personalities and I were surrounded by a vast number of persons in an arena. Unfortunately, once I had become conscious of this leading group of four, my circumstances became so difficult that I lost them.

"I must add here that since my life has been so full of emotional events, it is surprising that I have ever had any psychic abilities at all. For the most part, I find that emotionalism destroys clairvoyance and clairaudience. That the etheric personalities attempt to get through I feel sure, but there must by many difficulties on both sides—particularly on this one.

"And so I lost contact, but that wasn't surprising. In mid-June 1944, the great bombardment of London and southern Britain began."

Angelic Beings and Spiritual Guides

For several years now I have been collecting accounts from serious-minded men and women who are convinced that they have had personal interaction with angelic beings or spirit guides. Certain of these individuals have testified that they have received both supportive energy and protection from benevolent entities who have served as guardians.

Humankind in general has always believed in unseen intelligences inhabiting the invisible world. The holy books of nearly all religions inform their followers that such spiritual entities do exist and that they thrive in close proximity to our own world.

There is no question that in the Old and New Testaments angels are considered as beings concerned with the material affairs of Earth. They wrestle with stubborn shepherds, guide wanderers lost in the wilderness to oases, free the persecuted from fiery furnaces and dank prisons. Jesus, himself, was led, defended, and given strength by angels.

In recent history and in contemporary times, angels and spirit guides have appeared to soldiers, statesmen, doctors, businessmen—even to lawmen and gunfighters of the Old West.

Sheriff Slaughter's Guardian Angel

Contrary to popular Western mythology, Wyatt Earp did not clean up Tombstone Territory. The controversial Mr. Earp, in spite of his secure position in the legends of the West as a gallant lawman, was a gambler, a racketeer, and a part-time road agent who made a profit by dealing on both sides of the law. The fiction of Earp as the virtuous defender of law and order was largely the creation of Ned Buntline, a prolific dime-novel writer.

When Wyatt, his brothers, and his pal, Doc Holliday, left Tombstone after the famous gunfight at the OK Corral, the Arizona community was far from "clean." If anything, crime was more rampant than before the Earp regime.

The man who pinned on a tin star and really mopped up the territory was "Texas" John Slaughter. Slaughter was quick with his wits, fast on the draw with his pearl-handled revolver, and doggedly determined to make Tombstone a decent city. Texas John had two important advantages over all the previous lawmen who had tackled Tombstone and failed—he had finely honed sixth sense and an active guardian angel.

Slaughter had been a successful rancher before he moved to Arizona and took on the job of sheriff for Tombstone Territory, so he was accustomed to rubbing up against tough hombres.

"I've got a guardian angel who protects me," he would tell well-meaning friends when they sought to caution him about his reckless and daring life-style. "My angel keeps these owl hoots and gunslicks from even denting me. I'll die in bed when I'm good and ready."

The Angel's Warning "Buzz"

Once, when Texas John was riding his famous gray horse on his way to buy some cattle, he received the warning "buzz" from his guardian angel, which told him that he was approaching danger. Whenever he got the signal from his invisible guide, he never argued.

He sat atop his horse for a time, assessing the message he had received. Danger lay ahead, the communication assured him, so he decided to ride into the town of Tubac. Here he visited with a storekeeper until his angel sent him the "all-clear" signal.

Later that day, three gunslingers who worked for Curly Bill Brocius, Texas John's archenemy, rode into Tubac. Over beers in the saloon, they were overheard to be cursing their bad luck. It seemed that Curly Bill had learned of Slaughter's cattle-buying trip and had sent the three of them to lie in ambush for him.

"We squatted out there in that boiling sun until we felt like dried-out venison," one of them growled to a local tough. "Curly Bill is going to be mad, but we ain't no Apache. We couldn't lay there in that sun waiting for Texas John until Christmas!"

One night Slaughter and his wife had attended a social function at a neighbor's and were driving home after dark in their buckboard. Mrs. Slaughter saw her husband cock his head in the bright moonlight.

"What do you hear, John?" she asked.

Slaughter handed her the reins and unholstered his gun. "My angel just sent me the buzz," he told her.

"We are going to be a whole lot safer if you drive and I have my gun in my hand." Mrs. Slaughter had barely finished speaking when a horseman emerged from the shadows, and the angry features of rustler Ike Clanton were distinguishable in the moonlight. The tough old patriarch of the outlaw clan had sworn to kill the troublesome sheriff, and he rode out in front of the buckboard with his revolver already drawn.

But when Ike saw the moonlight glinting off the six-gun in the fast-shooting Slaughter's hand, he turned his horse and rode on without speaking a word or firing a shot.

Get Away From That Window

The lawman's sixth sense did not lose its effectiveness with age. On the evening of May 4, 1921, when Tombstone, the Clantons, and Curly Bill had become the stuff of memories, the old frontier sheriff got his angel's danger signal while sitting in his dining room reading the evening paper.

"It was as if I heard my faithful guardian angel screaming right in my ear," Slaughter said later. "There was just a bit of the old buzz, then I heard his voice shout at me: 'Get away from that open window and get your gun!'"

Puzzled but ever heedful of the adviser who had consistently gotten him out of tough scrapes alive, Slaughter set down his newspaper and literally sprang to his feet.

He was in the bedroom buckling on his gun belt when two shots rang out and killed his foreman, Jes Fisher.

Later, when the four ranch hands involved in the plot were arrested, they confessed that Slaughter was also to have been killed.

One of the conspirators had been drawing a bead on Texas John, who sat reading in front of a window, when Slaughter suddenly jumped to his feet and moved quickly out of sight. Another instant over the newspaper and the old lawman, an easy target in the light from the reading lamp, would have been dead.

"It's like I've always told you," Slaughter said to his friends. "My guardian angel told me years ago that I would die in bed. Once again he sent the warning in time so that that bushwhacker's bullet never found me. He isn't going to let anything happen to me until it is my time to go."

The time finally came for John Horton Slaughter in 1922, when he passed away—the victim of a stroke, not a gunman's bullet.

The Mystery of the Spirit Guide

The idea of a spirit guide dates back to antiquity. Socrates furnishes us with the most notable example in ancient times of a man whose subjective mind was able to communicate with his objective mind by direct speech stimulus. Socrates referred to this voice as his *daemon,* not to be confused with *demon,* a possessing or negative energy; *daemon* is better translated as "guardian angel." The philosopher believed that the spirit guide kept vigil and warned him of approaching danger.

This phenomenon is experienced by many people throughout the course of their lives. While some truly feel the guide is an independent spiritual being, others believe the phenomenon to be another aspect of ESP that may lie latent in each of us and come into play when we are threatened with danger, when we are ill, or when we are in some way facing a personal crisis.

The subjective, transcendent level of mind may dramatize a danger warning in the voice of an extraneous personality. In other cases the subjective mind of an individual may clairaudiently contact its own objective level, as in the instances of those people, like Socrates, who claim to have a personal "daemon."

A medium, therefore, may, on one level of the mind, telepathically gain information from the subjective mind of a sitter with whom he is in rapport. The knowledge itself, however, may reach both the medium and the sitter at the same time through the clairaudient manifestation of the "spirit guide."

I have in my files numerous instances wherein one's own transcendent level of mind has "called" to the objective level and caused it to act in order to avert danger.

A close friend claims that he is always awakened by the gently calling voice of his mother whenever it is important for him to be up early to prepare a vital brief in his law practice. He never bothers to set an alarm clock, no matter how crucial it may be that he rise at a certain time. He is confident that his "mother's voice" will not fail to call him in plenty of time.

This would make an impressive and touching illustration of a mother's continuing interest in her son if it were not for the fact that my friend's mother is still very much alive. His transcendent level of mind seems to have chosen a voice that will rouse the objective personality efficiently and with a feeling of security.

A student of mine once told me that she often heard a voice calling her name when it was time for her to begin her nightly studies. The voice had no recognizable tonal qualities and seemed neutral in gender as well. The function of the voice seemed to be a Jiminy Cricket–type voice of the conscience that would summon her from frivolity to a session with the books.

One time, when she was having difficulty getting to work and had decided instead to write a letter to her fiancé, the voice became externalized and called her name so loudly that her roommate was awakened from a catnap.

Asking Irene Hughes About Guides and Mediumship

Irene Hughes is an intelligent, articulate woman, as well as a perceptive, highly accurate medium and psychic-sensitive, and she has the forthright answers for any sincere seeker of additional information in regard to her psychic abilities.

Irene, from what source do you consider your abilities to be derived? By that I mean, do you feel that they come from God, from guiding spirits, from your unconscious?

Irene Hughes: First of all, the gift of intuition is one of God's original gifts to all men. I have had mystical experiences in communication with a divine intelligence whom I call God, and I also gain many of my talents through telepathic communication and through assistance from spirit intelligences. You know, of course, about Kaygee, my Japanese spirit guide and teacher.

Do you feel that your psychic or mediumistic gifts are compatible with the principal bodies of organized religion?

Irene: Oh, I definitely feel that my psychic gifts are compatible with organized religion, but I also believe that these gifts transcend certain organized beliefs.

Do you believe that there is a part of man that survives physical death?

Irene: Yes, it is the soul or spirit, that which is "within" man, unseen but felt.

Irene, what is your understanding of "heaven" and the afterlife?

Irene: Well, I certainly do not visualize any geographical location. What is commonly called *heaven* is, I believe, a state of consciousness both here and after physical death. The afterlife is another experience in the evolution and growth of the soul as it reaches toward Christ-like perfection.

I have found that when symbols come—or impressions of any sort—I have a certain and very definite feeling that sometimes develops into a deep knowing and indicates beyond doubt that the impression is accurate.

Do you have vivid dreams? And are you able to exercise a certain amount of control over them?

Irene: I sometimes have extremely vivid dreams, but I have never tried to exercise control over my dreams other than asking that I should remember them.

What do you consider to be your basic trait, Irene? How do you see yourself?

Irene: I believe that I am basically honest and extremely loyal to my beliefs and to my friends. I also feel that I am reasonably generous. I feel that I have a sincere spiritual love for most human beings. I respect all people because of my belief that the Christ consciousness is within each of us.

What one thing do you believe so fervently that you would act on that belief without hesitation in a moment of crisis?

Irene: Because I believe that each being is guided from within in moments of crisis, I would act according to the guidance that was given to me at that moment, depending upon the crisis and the guidance given. When I say *guidance given*, I believe that this guidance would come from the original survival abilities instilled through, or within, the faculties of perception, which come from acknowledging God.

The Man Who Became a Millionaire by Listening to Ghosts

Before Arthur Edward Stilwell died on September 26, 1928, he had built the Kansas City Southern Railroad; the Kansas City Northern Connecting Railroad; the Kansas City, Omaha and Eastern; the Kansas City, Omaha and Orient; the Pittsburg and Gulf Railroad; and the Port Arthur Ship Canal.

This hardheaded, practical businessman had been responsible for the laying of over twenty-five hundred miles of double-track railroad and had founded forty towns. His vast empire employed over a quarter of a million people and extended itself from the vast railroad network to pecan farming, banking, land development, and mining.

In his spare time he wrote and published thirty books, nineteen of which were novels, among them the well-known *Light That Never Failed*.

Although his contemporaries hailed him as a genius with unstoppable luck, Arthur Stilwell never took any of the credit for his impressive accomplishments. Throughout his long and prosperous career as a modern-day Midas, Stilwell protested that he was but an instrument of his spirit guides.

According to Stilwell, his mentors from the spirit world had been responsible for every financial investment and decision that he'd ever made, and had dictated every word in his thirty volumes, numerous articles, and many motion-picture scenarios.

A "Highly Personal" Relationship with Spirit Guides

"My case is not all that unusual," Stilwell would point out to those who met his claims with incredulity. "Socrates, greatest of the Greek philosophers, used to give credit to his 'Daemon.' Joan of Arc changed history by listening to her spirit guides."

To Arthur Stilwell the relationship he shared with his spirit friends was a highly personal one, and other than acknowledging the essential role they played in his career, he never identified them beyond stating that his spirit circle was made up of the spirits of three engineers, a poet, and two writers. The millionaire's interaction with the world of the supernatural was as real and as vital to him as his association with his earthly circle of friends, which included Henry Ford, George Westinghouse, and Charles Schwab.

Sir Arthur Conan Doyle, creator of Sherlock Holmes, once said that Arthur Stilwell "had greater and more important psychic experiences than any man of this generation."

His psychic experiences began when Stilwell was a boy on his father's farm in eastern Indiana.

Since his early childhood Arthur had been a sensitive lad who was given to much daydreaming. By the time he was in his early teens he had acquired the ability to fall into trances and receive advice, admonitions, and prophecies from his advisers in the spirit circle.

On his fifteenth birthday young Arthur was told that he would be married in four years' time to a girl named Genevieve Wood.

"But I don't even know any girl by such a name," the teenager protested.

After the spirits had finished giving their counsel and had

faded back into the night shadows, young Arthur rose and wrote the name down in his diary.

Four years later, just after his nineteenth birthday, he found himself dancing with a pretty girl at a church festival. When she told him her name was Jenny Wood, he remembered the prophecy and the name he had recorded in his diary. Within a few weeks Genevieve Wood and Arthur Stilwell were married.

Even the most faithful disciple of Horatio Alger's rags-to-riches romanticism easily would have been persuaded to put his money on someone other than Arthur Stilwell to become a millionaire. He was a farm boy who had barely made it through high school, had acquired a wife while he was still a teenager, and had now gained employment as a clerk with a trucking firm.

How many trucking company clerks became millionaires?

But how many clerks have the benefit of counsel from a spirit circle?

Inspiring Voices from Out of the Darkness

In the darkness they came to him. "Go west and build a railroad," they repeated night after night.

Young Stilwell protested. He knew nothing of railroads and nothing of high finance. He was just a farm boy.

But still the ghostly voices beleaguered him. They pestered him so much that he had to sleep in a separate bedroom so that he would not disturb his wife.

In the early days of their marriage Arthur did not dare discuss his invisible advisers with Jenny for fear that she would think him strange. After assuring her that all was well between them, Arthur gave some feeble explanation of why he must sleep in his own bedroom.

GHOSTS AMONG US

It was a practice Stilwell would continue for the rest of their long married life, but as success followed success, eventually he was able to confide in Jenny and explain the necessity of his being able to "confer" with his guides in solitude.

Go West and Build a Railroad

Yielding at last to the demands of his spirit circle, Stilwell moved to Kansas City, where he managed to find work with various brokerage firms. With the aid of his ghostly allies he mastered the finer points of finance. Before he was twenty-six, he had built his first railroad, the Kansas City Belt Line.

Stilwell had found no difficulty borrowing the money from bankers, and upon completing the line a month ahead of schedule, he found that suddenly he had been transformed from a forty-dollar-a-month clerk to a man who owned a railroad worth millions.

Later Stilwell recorded that during this period of his life, which required more nerve and self-confidence than even the most bold Indiana farm boy could muster, he had relied heavily on the advice and aid of his spirit friends. Often when an engineering problem had him stumped, he would slip into a trance and awaken the next morning to find that the drawing board now bore the solution. These notes and drawings, according to Stilwell, were never in his own handwriting.

Uniting Midwestern Farmers With the Ocean

Perhaps the most dramatic prophecy of Stilwell's spirit circle occurred when they advised Arthur to build a railroad line from Kansas City to the Gulf of Mexico.

Stilwell was immediately impressed with the wisdom of such a move. He realized that such a linkup would unite the Midwestern farmers with ocean steamships. He began at once, putting the plan into motion.

Galveston, Texas, seemed to be the logical terminus of this new branch line, and Stilwell completely immersed himself in the new project. For the first time in his life he became so absorbed in a new undertaking that he seemed to block out the visitation of his spirit friends.

"I made the very human mistake of depending upon myself and upon tangible things in my hour of need, forgetting the spiritual aid which was waiting and ready," Stilwell wrote later.

Then, suddenly, as if the spirits had devised a last-resort method of forcing their fleshy protége to slow down a bit, Stilwell became ill.

Work on the railroad came to a halt, but Arthur was able to reestablish contact with his faithful spirit circle.

"You must not let the new railroad line go to Galveston," Stilwell was told.

"But where else would I possibly locate the terminus?" Arthur said with a frown, putting the question to his ethereal tutors bluntly.

"That should be no problem for a millionaire. Build a new city. Name it Port Arthur."

Arthur snorted. "People will not only say that I am mad, they also will say that I am vain."

"Let them say what they will. Nothing your detractors can say will equal the disaster that will take place in Galveston if you allow your railroad to establish its terminus in that city. Your life's work will be ruined, and thousands of lives will be lost."

Stilwell stirred uneasily in the bed where he was holding

this "conference." He asked his guides exactly what they meant by uttering such ominous words.

A Cinematic Projection of the Future

"Look here," he was commanded, "and you will see for yourself."

There, on his bedroom wall, a misty picture of the city of Galveston began to swirl and waver until at last it took form with the clarity of a steropticon slide. This most miraculous "picture" showed people walking the city's streets. The focus suddenly shifted to the docks of the seaport. Stevedores hustled up gangplanks with cargo; cranes dropped tons of wheat into open holds. Then the sky over the ocean became dark and troubled. From far out at sea a great tidal wave rose out of the waters like a brutal, hulking beast of vengeance sent by an angry Neptune. The monstrous wave gained momentum as it rolled faster and faster toward the shore and the seaport.

It flung itself on the city of Galveston, the fury of nature's power gone beserk. The Texas city was literally crushed, its people drowning.

At last the horrible vision faded from the bedroom wall. Arthur Stilwell lay in his bed, damp with perspiration and totally convinced by the demonstration his spirit guides had just presented.

"I shall build Port Arthur," he assured the grim features of the ghostly prophets.

Stilwell returned from his sickbed completely rejuvenated. His first official action was to order the change in the course of the new railroad line.

Port Arthur was staked out in a vacant cow pasture. The

precise location had been marked on a map by Stilwell's spirit circle.

"The man is insane!" Stilwell's critics shouted when his plans were announced.

Gavelston's business associations and citizens groups violently protested the railroad baron's change of plans. They were ignorant of the vision of the terrible tidal wave that would crush their city. The only vision they were concerned about was the one that showed them losing thousands of dollars in profits to a city that had not been built yet.

Cautiously Stilwell spoke to them of his vision of the great tidal wave that would destroy Galveston. As he feared, this pronouncement angered Galveston's emissaries even more.

"It's bad enough that Stilwell has betrayed us," they grumbled, "but now he has the unmitigated gall to tell us that he has changed his plans because of a bad dream!"

Then there were those who had hoped to profit from the sale of condemned lands along the original site of Stilwell's proposed railroad. These men joined with Stilwell's enemies in Wall Street and brought the fight into Congress.

Port Arthur Rises From Cow Pasture and Swamp

But Stilwell, with the constant encouragement of his spiritual advisers, held his ground and continued to finance both the completion of the new line and the construction of the new city.

Several years later an official ceremony christened Port Arthur, the terminus for the Kansas City Southern Railroad. What had once been a useless swamp had been transformed into a canal equal to the width and depth of the Suez. What had once been a cow pasture was now a new and proud seaport where steamers could dock while the waiting trainloads of Midwestern corn, wheat, and oil were transferred to their holds.

Only four days after the ceremonies that signaled the twin births of a railroad line and a seaport, the city of Galveston, Texas, was destroyed by a mammoth tidal wave that thundered over the Gulf Coast. The disaster occurred exactly at the time that had been revealed to Arthur Stilwell by his spirit guides, and exactly as he had predicted for the past several years.

The huge tidal wave that smashed into Galveston was responsible for one of the greatest catastrophes in American history, but by the time it reached Port Arthur, across Sabine Lake, it was as mild as a ripple in a pond. Once again Arthur Stilwell's spirit circle had given impressive proof of the validity of their existence, as well as their unerring accuracy.

Because Stilwell had heeded the advice of his spirit mentors, Port Arthur served as a relief center for the striken populace of its neighboring city.

Stilwell's own personal fortune was increased many times over. If he had followed his original plan and built his railroad terminal in Galveston, his empire would have been destroyed. Those who had once mocked him as a fool for erecting a city in the middle of a cow pasture when an established seaport stood eagerly awaiting the commerce of his railroad line were now hailing him as a genius, a visionary, and the luckiest man in the world.

Stilwell was quick to point out that he had had more than luck on his side.

As Arthur Stilwell became internationally known as one of America's greatest empire builders, more and more people began to question him about his spirit guides. Stilwell was never one to theorize about his "friends." He felt no compulsion to attempt to explain how he was able to interact with the spirit world or why those in the etheric realm should choose to bother themselves with the concerns of those still clothed in flesh.

An Empire Built by Etheric Advisers

Stilwell never made a single effort to answer the questions of the skeptics. The multimillionaire felt that the empire he had built with the aid of his spirit mentors offered the best kind of evidence of their existence.

Stilwell did, however, reveal how he was able to contact the members of his spirit circle.

"I lie down in bed alone in a dark room," he once told a business associate. "I focus my mind on my immediate problem and allow myself to drift off into a sort of half sleep. I offer no resistance to any outside influence. I suppose the state is very similar to that of a coma, but even though I am nearly unconscious, every plan, diagram, chart, or map which is revealed to me during those moments is indelibly etched in my memory."

According to Stilwell, his spirit guides did not express themselves with any sense of time. Past, present, and future were all one to them. They seemed to have access to all knowledge issued to them by the Absolute Power and dictated their suggestions to Stilwell with utmost authority.

Stilwell lived into his eighties and entertained himself in his twilight years by writing. This still left him plenty of time to manage his sprawling railroad empire and his varied commercial interests.

He died clutching his wife's hand, confidently telling Jenny that he, himself, would soon be a member in good standing in the Spirit Circle.

▪ EPILOGUE ▪

The Enigma of the Ghosts Among Us

In spite of accounts as astonishing as those of Arthur Stilwell, serious investigators of the paranormal continue to ask if these mediumistic phenomena are truly evidence of the direct interaction between humans and discarnate spirits, or if they are representative of our own transcendent power of mind. Are the men and women who believe they are in contact with the surviving essences of the deceased truly communicating with spirits, or are they receiving information from a higher aspect of themselves?

Modern men and women seek the answers to the mystery of life beyond the grave as earnestly as did our ancestors. Surely the persistent sightings of ghosts among us provide us with continual clues that there is something within each of us that does conquer death.

I have stated my opinion that I believe the majority of haunting phenomenon to represent dynamic memory patterns that are somehow impressed upon an environment. We cannot interact with those ghostly vibrations, any more than we can interact with the electronic images that appear on our television or motion-picture screens.

On the other hand, there are numerous accounts indicating that intelligences exist that somehow move and shape ghostly forms. Whether these intelligences are discarnate beings, surviving spirits, or multidimensional entities constitutes a presently impenetrable enigma—one that I have endeavored to present objectively and free of dogma.

It is my observation that the phenomenon we label as ghosts appears to manifest more often when the receiver of such a visitation is in an altered state of consciousness. That is why so many accounts of ghostly encounters sound very much like dreams. The experiences have, in effect, taken place while the witness was in a dreamlike state.

While investigating certain haunting cases I have often hypnotized the witnesses so that I might better obtain a clue as to what actually happened during the experience. When hypnosis is successful, it enables us to speak directly to the unconscious, rather than to the conscious, which employs many screening devices at many levels.

In some instances I believe the process of hypnosis enabled me to see that we were dealing more with a haunted mind than a restless spirit. In other cases it may have been the troubled psyche that reactivated or set into motion a residue of festering memory, the last earthly pain of a tormented mind submitting to suicide or murder. In yet other investigations I discovered allegedly benign entities who were very different from the manner in which they presented themselves to trusting humans.

I have come to preach caution when it comes to people expressing their desire to communicate with ghosts. As it warns in the Bible, "test the spirits" and do not be deceived. I have come to accept an objective, external reality for certain entities—both positive and negative. And when these entities do communicate with us, it seems that they utilize both the unconscious and certain archetypal images in order to accomplish their transmission of inspiration—or fear.

Basically it seems to me that the ghosts among us are but another manifestation of a Greater Reality that is designed to demonstrate to us that there is an unseen world with powers and principalities beyond the boundaries of conventional reality. The lesson of such manifestations is not to revert to superstition but to progress to a higher state of consciousness and awareness. The secret always is to learn to live in wisdom and in spiritual and physical balance.

"I have seen the future of horror . . . and its name is Clive Barker." —Stephen King

BOOKS BY *NEW YORK TIMES* BESTSELLING AUTHOR

CLIVE BARKER

__ **THE DAMNATION GAME** 1-55773-113-6/$4.95

There are things worse than death. There are games so seductively evil, no gambler can resist. Joseph Whitehead dared to challenge the dark champion of life's ultimate game. Now he has hell to pay.

CLIVE BARKER'S BOOKS OF BLOOD

No collection of horror stories can compare to Clive Barker's gruesome spinechillers. "Clive Barker redefines the horror tale in his Books of Blood, bringing new beauty to ghastliness and new subtleties to terror." --*Locus*

__ **VOLUME ONE**   0-425-09347-6/$3.95
__ **VOLUME TWO**   0-425-08389-6/$3.95
__ **VOLUME THREE**   0-425-08739-5/$3.95

Check book(s). Fill out coupon. Send to:

BERKLEY PUBLISHING GROUP
390 Murray Hill Pkwy., Dept. B
East Rutherford, NJ 07073

NAME_____
ADDRESS_____
CITY_____
STATE_____ ZIP_____

PLEASE ALLOW 6 WEEKS FOR DELIVERY.
PRICES ARE SUBJECT TO CHANGE
WITHOUT NOTICE.

POSTAGE AND HANDLING:
$1.00 for one book, 25¢ for each additional. Do not exceed $3.50.

BOOK TOTAL $____
POSTAGE & HANDLING $____
APPLICABLE SALES TAX $____
(CA, NJ, NY, PA)
TOTAL AMOUNT DUE $____

PAYABLE IN US FUNDS.
(No cash orders accepted.)

by the *New York Times* bestselling author who terrified millions with THE KEEP...
"It has true fear in it!" — Peter Straub, bestselling author of *Koko*

f. paul wilson
reborn

A return to *The Keep*'s vampiric evil

A Nobel Prize-winning genetic researcher has died—now his vast fortune, a Victorian mansion, and darkest secrets will be passed on to Jim Stevens. An orphan, Jim hopes the inheritance is a clue to his unknown origins. But his family and friends are plagued with apocalyptic warnings: "The Evil One is coming." And Jim's wife is about to give birth.
___REBORN F. Paul Wilson 0-515-10343-8/$4.95

For Visa and MasterCard orders call: 1-800-631-8571

FOR MAIL ORDERS: CHECK BOOK(S). FILL OUT COUPON. SEND TO:

BERKLEY PUBLISHING GROUP
390 Murray Hill Pkwy., Dept. B
East Rutherford, NJ 07073

NAME_____
ADDRESS_____
CITY_____
STATE_____ZIP_____

PLEASE ALLOW 6 WEEKS FOR DELIVERY.
PRICES ARE SUBJECT TO CHANGE WITHOUT NOTICE.

POSTAGE AND HANDLING:
$1.00 for one book, 25¢ for each additional. Do not exceed $3.50.

BOOK TOTAL	$ ____
POSTAGE & HANDLING	$ ____
APPLICABLE SALES TAX (CA, NJ, NY, PA)	$ ____
TOTAL AMOUNT DUE	$ ____

PAYABLE IN US FUNDS.
(No cash orders accepted.)